WHEN THIS BELL RINGS

For the readers and the writers and all the lovers of stories.
And for Ashleigh, because I accidentally left her out last time.
— A R

First published in 2020
by Walker Books Australia Pty Ltd
Locked Bag 22, Newtown
NSW 2042 Australia
www.walkerbooks.com.au

A catalogue record for this
book is available from the
National Library of Australia

ISBN: 978 1760651 94 7

Typeset in Manticore
Printed and bound in Australia by Griffin Press

10 9 8 7 6 5 4 3 2 1

WHEN THIS BELL RINGS

Allison Rushby

WALKER BOOKS
AND SUBSIDIARIES
LONDON • BOSTON • SYDNEY • AUCKLAND

A book is a heart that only beats in the chest of another.
– REBECCA SOLNIT

IN the sea of dull shoes, I watch for the scarlet boots.

Leather lace-ups, shiny patent heels, scuffed sneakers. Black, brown, blue, boring. None of them that brilliant flash of colour against the grey pavement. None of them attached to *her* feet.

It's already 4:32 pm.

Maybe she's not coming?

From the desk in my basement room I keep staring up at street level. Every day, at exactly 4:30 pm she exits her townhouse and turns right, walking past my window.

Her name is Edie St Clair and she is a famous author. Just about everyone has read her graphic novels, or at least seen the movies.

Edie St Clair lives next door to me in Chester Square. Chester Square is full of rich people who live in fancy white townhouses. We aren't rich, but Edie St Clair is. The family my mother works for is also rich. She's a housekeeper. Each week, it is my mother's job to organise flowers for people who will never see them, and arrange cleaners for an already clean house. At Christmas time, the drawing room is redecorated and filled with a real tree and presents. The house holds its breath, its glassy eyes wide open. Hopeful.

The family never comes.

I live with my mother in a small apartment in the basement of the townhouse. That's where I draw Edie St Clair's characters. They're all I ever draw. I've been drawing them so long, they are good. *Very* good. I can say that, because I'm not good at many things.

Like reading.

Writing.

Maths.

Okay, all subjects, except for art.

At school there is too much reading. Too much writing. So, I draw. When I draw, the noise of the world goes away. I get in trouble for drawing. For not paying attention. Sometimes I wonder if it's like that for Edie St Clair, too. If everything is quiet and still when she draws.

One day later . . .

I know everything about Edie St Clair. I know that she drinks lots of tea (Darjeeling). She eats fruit toast with butter and a dash of cinnamon every morning for breakfast, and salmon with salad for lunch. She loves black clothes, red shoes and jewel-coloured scarves. She has a black cat called Ink who hates everybody but her. She has published nine books.

I know her tenth book is due next week.

I know this is why the journalists wait in front of her house.

I know this is why her feet run past my window now, instead of walk.

Two days later

There are more journalists now. They crowd the pavement. One of them spots me at my desk.

He crouches, holding onto the iron railings. His eyes light up when he sees what I'm drawing. He stands, opens the wrought-iron gate. Takes a step or two down the curved stairs towards my open window.

"Hey there!" he says. "Do you know Edie St Clair?"

His question is like a truth kick to my stomach.

I want to say "yes", but instead I have to shake my head.

I only *think* I know Edie St Clair.

Edie St Clair doesn't even know I exist.

"Come up and have a chat," the journalist says.

I don't look up from my drawing again.

Eventually I hear his shoes plod back up the stairs.

The man's visit makes me think. All those journalists – they *like* the fact that Edie St Clair is struggling to finish book ten. I think that's sad. Why does the world enjoy hearing about someone's failure more than their success?

What if all Edie St Clair needs is one person outside her house with a sign that says, "You can do it!" or "We're all behind you!" or something like that? I don't want Edie St Clair to fail. I want her to finish her series. I need that book. I can already imagine myself admiring its fancy display in the bookshop window. Lining up to buy it at midnight. Opening up the brown paper bag to sniff its delicious inky, papery goodness. Listening to the crack of the hardcover spine as I turn to the first page, desperate to start reading and at the same time worried that the final page will come too quickly.

What if none of that ever happens?

It has to happen.

I have to make it happen.

Maybe . . . maybe I could help her in some way?

Once the idea enters my head, I can't seem to let go of it. I have to let Edie St Clair know I'm down here. Waiting for that final book.

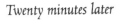

Twenty minutes later

I know what I'm going to do.

I'm finally going to talk to Edie St Clair. I'm going to give her a drawing. And I'm going to tell her I can't wait to see what happens in the next book.

Problem: I can't decide which drawing to give her.

I have hundreds. So many favourites. I mostly draw Kit, Wilf and Bes – Edie St Clair's most famous characters. They are the heroes of the *London of the Bells* series. They are all half faerie and half human. They are also my best friends. I stare at the drawings strewn across my desk, all of them sketched in strong black lines. I stare at them until they don't look like drawings any more, but more like the people who exist in my head – the ones I make up stories about, just like Edie St Clair does. I know it sounds silly to call them my best friends, but why not? I spend all my spare time with them. They are as real to me as real people. I even talk to them.

Actually, that's not a bad idea.

I close my eyes.

"Hey, guys! Which drawing should I give Edie St Clair?" I ask them.

"The one that's so amazing, so special, so unlike every drawing that has ever come before it that on viewing it every single one of the problems in Edie St Clair's life will instantly disappear, and she'll finish book ten in five minutes flat," a voice answers.

I swivel in my seat, my eyes still closed.

It's Bes, of course, in human form. She is small, brown, and hard as a little walnut. Bes's mother was a hyster sprite. Because of this, she can shapeshift into a tiny bird called a sand martin. But no wings are in sight now. Instead, her two arms are crossed in front of her as she leans against my bedroom wall.

"Oh, I have a bunch of drawings like that. You'll have to help me choose one." I don't take the bait. Bes is tough because she has to be. She's suffered the most in the London of the Bells. Her sisters died in book four and book six. Lots of people say they won't read Edie St Clair's final book because they believe that Bes is going to be killed off.

"You really expect us to decide something like this on an empty stomach?" Wilf appears on the other side of the room. As usual, his dirty red beanie is half-hanging off his head. He makes his way around my bed and trips on my school backpack as he goes. His stubby greenish arms dart out to stop his fall and he cracks a leg on the bedpost. He cries out in pain, rubbing his hairy half-hobgoblin shin and hopping the rest of the way over to Bes. "We'll need tea. Some cake. Biscuits, too, if you've got them. At the very least, toast. Not that there's really a decision to make. We all know it'll have to be that one." He points to a drawing stuck to my wall.

It's a picture of himself, of course.

"You're never going to change, are you?" Kit appears.

"That's why people love me," Wilf says.

Bes snorts. "Well, it's not for your looks or charm, that's for sure."

Kit doesn't join the others, but comes over to stand at my desk. He begins to flick through my pile of drawings. I watch as a lock of his iridescent hair falls forward and he pushes it back behind one ear. Kit's mother was an asrai – a water faerie – and Kit shares her features, tall and willowy with the lightest of light green eyes. But I know better than to say how good looking he is out loud. If I did, he'd likely run off for a quick dip in the Thames and come out covered in stinking mud, just so I'd have to take my words back.

Flick, flick, flick.

"You can really draw." He finally places the pile back down on the desk. "But it's not up to us. You know which one it needs to be. Trust in yourself."

I open my eyes.

Kit's right.

I get up from my desk and pluck the drawing from the wall.

This one.

It's a drawing of Kit himself. He's sitting on some stone watermen's stairs, looking out over the swirling grey Thames. Kit needs to be near the water, because of his asrai roots. There's a little bit of everything in this drawing – sadness, hope, a feeling of yesterday and tomorrow.

Yes.

I'm going to give Edie St Clair the drawing and I'm going to tell her I believe in her. She needs to know how much everyone needs this book.

At exactly 4:29 pm, I exit our apartment.

I climb the steep stone steps to the pavement, my hand sliding along the black iron railing. There are even more journalists waiting now. They juggle coffee cups, poke at phones, and jostle each other, trying to get the best spot in front of Edie St Clair's townhouse.

I wait behind the small iron gate at the top of our steps.

"Hello again!"

I look up to see the journalist who spoke to me earlier.

He bends down so his head is at the same height as mine. "Hey, seeing you're here, why don't you tell me a bit about your neighbour?"

"Right, you lot, back up," someone barks. It's a police officer. He's standing by Edie St Clair's front door, which has just opened a crack. "Give the lady some room."

The journalists grumble, but they move to create a path.

Edie St Clair wastes no time. She exits the townhouse and takes off. She crosses the road. Runs down the opposite pavement. She coughs, then coughs again. It's a rattling cough that comes from deep inside her. It sounds painful, and makes me clutch my own chest.

The journalists run after her. As they run, they shout questions. "Ms St Clair! Edie! Your book is due in just over a week. Is it true it's not finished?" And, "Is there any hope that you'll get your book in on time?" And, "Will this mean a delay in the scheduled publication date?" And, "What about the next movie? Will that be delayed, too?"

"Oi! No bothering her as she goes!" The police officer chases after them, all the way to the gates that lead into the private garden that runs the length of the street, opposite the townhouses. Edie St Clair enters the garden and disappears from view.

I stand very still on the stairs, the drawing hanging limp in my hand. I was going to give it to her. To talk to her. But I hadn't thought about how I would do that with all the journalists around. I see now that it was all just . . . a dream. Why did I ever think I could help her? Me. An absolute nobody, who copies her drawings.

A few of the journalists are looking at me. I want to fold myself up like a piece of origami, fold upon fold until I'm so small that I disappear from sight.

I take one step down towards our apartment, eager to return to the safety of my room. But something stops me from going any further. A little spark of courage. Am I really going to give up that easily? It's like Wilf says – if something feels too hard, it's probably worth doing. Quickly. Before you can change your mind.

So, before I can change my mind, I open the gate.

And I run across the road, just like Edie St Clair.

The journalists wait by the entrance to the private garden. The police officer keeps watch to make sure none of them climb over the spiky iron fence.

"Ah, it's my friend again." The journalist spots me. "She lives next door."

"That right?" The police officer gives me the eye, like I might also be a journalist. A very short one. "You going in there, too?" He jerks his thumb at the gate.

I pause. I don't know if I'm allowed inside the private garden. Yes, I live on Chester Square, but only because my mother works here. Not because I belong.

But then I remember something. I slide my hand into the pocket of my skinny black jeans and pull out a key. I stare at it. Did I put it there? I guess I must have, because it feels . . . right. Like it belongs.

"Well?" the police officer asks.

Frowning at him, I unlock the gate and enter the garden.

Inside, there are no journalists or police officers, only grass, trees, dappled light. Calm. Edie St Clair is nowhere in sight.

Until she is. Behind a tree, I spot a half-hidden green wooden bench. Beneath the bench, I see Edie St Clair's scarlet leather boots, one tucked neatly behind the other. I look down at my drawing, which is still in my hand.

I put the strange key in my pocket and smooth out the rumpled edge of the paper.

I walk towards her, thinking, *I can't do this*. I can't just walk up to Edie St Clair and talk to her. I mean, it's not like I haven't thought about it before, but I've always been scared I'd get it wrong, say something stupid. I want to turn around and scurry home, but I force my feet to keep stepping. One, two. I can't do this, but I'm going to. For once, just once, I want to feel like I've done something big and bold and brave, like the characters I'm always reading about.

I round the corner of the bench and her eyes lift to meet mine. Edie St Clair isn't old, but she isn't young, either. She wears a black dress and leggings and a bold scarf. These set off a short, dark bob and sparkling deep brown eyes that feel familiar somehow.

I thrust the drawing of Kit at her. I want to say something clever, but all my words are stuck to my teeth, like toffee.

She takes the paper from me. Looks at it.

"You're very talented, Tamsin," she says.

I gasp. "How do you know my name?"

Edie St Clair smiles up at me. "I've been expecting you. Sit." She pats the seat beside her. On her other side is a small new sketchpad and pencil.

I sit down. Slowly, carefully. I'm scared I might frighten her away like a skittish squirrel.

She passes me the sketchpad and pencil. "Now, draw me something different."

Easy, I think. But it isn't. I need to draw the perfect thing so Edie St Clair will like me. What should I draw? What shouldn't I draw? After too much time has passed, I force myself to start drawing in case my *not* drawing annoys her. I draw a line, then another and another and before I know it, a figure slowly starts to take shape.

"No!" Edie St Clair says, the moment she sees that the figure is Bes. She reaches out to clasp my hand. "I mean draw something for *you*. Just for you. Not something to please me."

I don't know what she means. I don't know what to draw. What to say. What to do. The pencil is motionless in my hand.

Edie St Clair spoke to me. Knew my name. Was interested in my drawing. And now I've gone and wrecked everything.

She sighs. Puts her hand out for the sketchpad and pencil.

Defeated, I give them to her. I go to get up.

"No, stay," she says. "Please stay."

I sit back down again, Edie St Clair watching me closely. The pencil twitches in her hand.

"Yes. Just like that. Don't move."

She begins to sketch. Edie St Clair is drawing me. Me! Maybe I haven't ruined everything after all.

Finally, there is a ripping sound. She passes me the piece of paper.

Edie St Clair's bold strokes detail a girl with short, dark hair. She is bending over a notebook, drawing. From the side, you can see that her thick brows are pushed together in concentration. I stare and stare and stare. It's so strange. I know it must be me, but it's like I've never seen myself before. But the best thing? If I squint, I can make myself believe Edie St Clair and I look a little bit alike. Dark hair, dark eyes, black clothes.

I'll keep this drawing forever.

Edie St Clair fishes another sketchpad out of her pocket. A second pencil. "Now," she says, "we draw together."

And that's exactly what we do.

I draw a rose. The bench. Some ivy. Edie St Clair's pretty boots.

"Can I keep that one?" she says to me. "I am particularly fond of these boots. I'm a firm believer in red shoes. They're good for the soul, if you'll pardon the pun."

I look down at my own shoes – scuffed red Converse – and I nod. I know exactly what she means.

I pass her the sketchpad.

"Oh, no. The sketchpad is yours," she says. "But I'd love the picture."

Carefully, I rip it out. Give it to her.

We sit in silence for a while.

"Thank you, Tamsin. That was a lovely afternoon," she says after some time. "Why don't we do it again tomorrow?"

WE meet in the garden the next day. The day after that, it rains. My mother – always busy – leaves me one of her notes to say Edie St Clair called. I've been invited to go and draw with her in her study.

I go next door to her townhouse. I have to push past the journalists, who ask a lot of questions. Everyone watches as I climb the one wide step that leads to her front door. There I pause, looking around me. I feel so small. Everything is too large. Too fancy. Too perfect. The gloss of the shiny black door, the polished brass of the lion's head knocker, the gleaming glass pendant light above my head. Before I can press the intercom button, the door opens. An older woman with a peach cardigan and a friendly smile greets me.

"Ah, Tamsin, is it? Edie's been expecting you. I'm Mrs Marchant, her housekeeper. Come along."

I step inside and Mrs Marchant closes the door behind me.

"If you wait here for just a moment, I'll fetch Edie for you."

Mrs Marchant bustles off down the hallway, leaving

me by myself. It doesn't feel right, being in Edie St Clair's house. It's not like my downstairs apartment with its worn carpet. Up here, the floors are cool grey marble. Everything matches. Every surface is smooth and shiny – lemon-fresh and highly polished.

"Hello, Tamsin." Edie makes her way down the hallway.

"Hel–" I see it before Edie does – the large black cat padding its way down the stairs in front of me. "Oh," I say. I've heard about Ink. That he's mean. That he doesn't like anyone in the whole world except Edie St Clair. A journalist once had to get stitches after trying to pat him.

Ink pauses on the stairs. He gazes at me with his big green eyes. And then he continues straight towards me.

I keep still, wondering if Edie St Clair will save me. But she doesn't. Instead, she looks on, as if curious to see what will happen.

When Ink reaches me, I wait for him to hiss. To swipe at me with his claws. But he doesn't. Instead, he butts his warm head against my leg. I wait a moment before reaching down and stroking his ears. Is this a trick? Will he wait until I'm comfortable with him and then scratch me?

But no. He only purrs and butts against my leg harder, asking for more.

"He . . . I . . . I think he likes me." I glance up at Edie St Clair.

"It would seem so." She turns away quickly. "Let's start." I'm forced to abandon Ink with a final pat and follow her along the hallway.

"Here we are." Edie St Clair gestures, opening the first door we come to. "This is my study."

I hesitate. This is where Edie St Clair works. To go in there would feel like . . . well, like spying.

She waves me inside and I finally move. The room is huge. It is not a normal study with a desk. A chair. A window. This room is long. The walls are covered in shelves. The shelves are filled with everything *London of the Bells*. Books, movie posters, figurines, board games, plush toys. The graphic novels take pride of place, lit up on a central shelf made of glass. I walk over to them. The purists would like this spotlit shelf. The purists claim to read only the graphic novels – the way the story was meant to be told.

People have a lot of opinions when it comes to *London of the Bells*.

When I look at the novelisations, Edie St Clair pounces. "And what do you think of those?"

"Um . . ." I don't know whether I should tell her, but then I remember she had problems at school as well. She didn't write the novelisations. She couldn't. "I haven't read them. I've listened to all the audiobooks, though."

"You're like me. The words jump about in front of your eyes, don't they?"

How did she know that?

"You know, at school they told me I was lazy. And stupid. But I wasn't lazy and stupid. I was – am – dyslexic, that's all. And I'm glad, because it means I've become good at other things to make up for it. You should know that. About me. About yourself."

I think she expects an answer. "Okay."

"I know school's tough. But you'll get through it."

As she speaks, a horrible feeling pulses through me. It's as if I'm actually in the classroom. Like they're right behind me, sniggering like they always seem to be.

"I know how it is. I know they laugh at you. But on the other side of your school years there will be a job you love and people you enjoy working with. Trust me."

I shiver, shaking off that classroom feeling. Shaking off how she seems to know exactly what I'm thinking. I don't know what to say. What she wants to hear.

For comfort and something to do, I reach for the shelf nearest me and pick up the graphic novel of book one. This is where everything began. I can feel Edie St Clair's eyes on me. She wants to talk more about our shared problem, I can feel it. To distract her, I turn the book over and act like I'm very busy reading the blurb.

"Read it aloud," Edie St Clair says.

I look up at her. I would never usually read aloud in front of someone, but I've practically memorised the words, so I know I won't stumble too badly. I also know this is a safe space. Edie will understand if I make a mistake.

The human and faerie worlds were never meant to mix. But the faerie folk found a way to bridge this divide – by using ravens as a connection.

Time saw the Ravens rise up, stealing faerie magic and making it their own, driving the folk deep underground. The Ravens then enslaved the humans of London by enchanting the fourteen great bells of the city, and cut London off from the rest of the world with an invisible wall.

Only the children of a human and a faerie are immune to the chimes of the bells. And only a few exist. As a rule, faeries of different clans do not work well together. But now they must find a way to come together to defeat the Ravens and separate two worlds that were never meant to be combined.

Ugh. How could I have got so many words wrong?

But Edie St Clair only smiles. "Lovely. Come on, then. Time to draw." She beckons me over to the large desk in the centre of the room.

I take one side. Edie St Clair takes the other.

"There's only one rule."

"Oh?" Something about the way she's looking at me tells me it's an important rule. Not some silly adult rule about keeping eraser shavings off the floor.

"We can draw anything but the London of the Bells."

I consider this for a moment. I suppose she wants to stop thinking about book ten.

"Okay," I say.

Edie St Clair wants to draw with me in her study.

Ink likes me.

Things are good.

Next step: get Edie St Clair to deliver that book on time.

IT keeps raining. And we keep drawing in Edie St Clair's study.

Over two long sessions, I fill sketchpad after sketchpad. Edie St Clair seems to have a limitless number of large sketchpads. As soon as I finish one, she pulls a fresh one out like magic. All I can think is how amazing it must be to be grown up and able to buy as many large sketchpads as you want. I draw birds with hats and aliens playing tennis and crazy cars of the future. Edie St Clair stares and stares at me.

It's almost like she's never seen someone draw before.

I work up the courage to ask her about it. "You must have drawn when you were my age," I say.

"Yes, I did. I drew just for me. I used to carry around a little sketchpad. And I would draw and draw and draw. It was bliss."

I put my pencil down. "But you draw now. All the time."

"Of course. But not for myself. Not for the sheer joy of it." Edie St Clair coughs a deep, chesty cough that rattles her lungs. "Sorry," she says, waving a hand. "You can't catch it."

I notice how thin she's become. She's really not well.

Before I can say anything, she continues. "The thing is, there are a lot of people I could let down if I draw just for myself."

I've wanted to ask her about this. About the journalists. About the next book.

"People are saying I haven't even started the book. But that's not true. I have – I'm up to the final scenes. But I'm stuck. So stuck . . ." Edie St Clair's head sinks into her hands.

There's a long silence that doesn't feel right. For the first time, I think about leaving.

"Tamsin?" She doesn't look up.

"Yes?"

"There's something I've got to tell you."

"There's a problem with the ending, isn't there?" I blurt out. "A big problem. Maybe . . . maybe I could help you figure it out?"

Her head snaps up, her eyes locking onto mine. "Everyone expects the book to end a certain way – with this huge final battle. And for a while I believed that's what should happen. I planned it all out. But now–" she pauses to cough again, "it simply doesn't feel right. But it's got to happen. I know it does. Did you know there are whole blogs devoted just to this ending? Who's going to die. Who's going to live."

I think about Bes.

"#saveBes," Edie St Clair says, as if sensing my thoughts again. How does she do that?

This is the hashtag that goes with the fan theory about Bes dying in the final book. Fans say it's not right. That she's an easy target. That it's not fair to keep hurting her just to make us feel. I know what they mean. Sometimes it feels as if Edie St Clair has been meaner to Bes than all the other characters combined. Bes is like a tender bruise that is cruelly kicked over and over again.

"The ending . . . it's all I can think about. I can't get away from it. No one will let me. All I'm asked about is this battle. That and Bes. If I'm spotted out at the movies, people tell me I should be writing. They remind me my book's almost due. They tell me I shouldn't go on holidays, or out for dinner with friends. They say I should exercise more. Look after myself better. That I've let myself get sick."

"It's not your fault you caught a cold. And they can't tell you what to do."

Edie shrugs. "You know what happened, of course. You know about all the . . . fuss with the end."

Of course I know. Who doesn't? It all started with the actor who plays Bes. A journalist asked her opinion about the next book– how would the ending play out? Would her character be killed off? She said she thought there'd be a massive final battle. That her character might not make it. They were just her opinions, but the world took them as the truth.

The film studio fired her for it.

Edie had been appalled – the actor was only fourteen. Edie had managed to have her reinstated, but the studio hadn't been happy about it.

I nod. "I know what happened. But the ending is yours to write. You don't owe anyone anything."

"Don't I?" Edie St Clair stares at her desk. All of a sudden, she thrusts her hand into her pocket and retrieves something – a key. She unlocks a little drawer in her desk and takes out another key. "Come with me. I think it's time I showed you something."

Edie St Clair is out of the study in a flash. I have to rush to follow her into the hallway. The light from the chandelier above provides the only illumination on the gloomy afternoon.

Again I get the feeling that I shouldn't be here. My steps slow. I want to go home.

"Edie?" I say in a small voice.

She doesn't look back, but stops halfway down the hall in front of a closed door. It's only as I reach her that I realise there shouldn't be a door here. There shouldn't be a room at all. Not even a cupboard.

She unlocks the door and pushes it open wide.

"Oh," I exhale, when I see what it is.

There, in front of me, is a whole other world.

IT is the *London of the Bells* series come to life. It is the world inside Edie St Clair's head.

I step in through the doorway and turn slowly, looking around.

It's a whole other townhouse. But it's nothing like the one we've just come from – showy and proper. This is something else entirely.

It is empty, except for the walls, which are full, because Edie St Clair has covered them from floor to ceiling. Her drawings dance across the walls, somehow seeming more alive than in the printed books. More real. As if this is where they truly belong. Some sections are sketchy and crossed out hurriedly, others are in beautiful detail, some even in colour.

It's insane.

An empty townhouse in expensive Belgravia used only for drawing on the walls.

I *love* it.

I spin. Drawings stretch out down the hallway. They rise up the staircase. Twisting and turning along the hallway, I lose my footing and bump into the wall.

When I focus on it, I see a scene from the end of book one. It's the one where Kit, Wilf and Bes are sent out on their first proper raid. They've been grouped together against their will and sent on a mission to regain control of the bell of Shoreditch. The threesome is hiding in what used to be an office, peering out at the soaring steeple of St Leonard's church through a window caked with dirt.

It's here, on this raid, that they figure out how to work as a team. It might not seem like a big scene, but after you've read the other books and you know what's coming, it's huge. It's full of the electricity of what's to come. What Kit, Wilf and Bes could achieve if they let go of who they think they are and open themselves up to who they could be. They defy mathematical logic – when it comes to them, one is more than three.

Leaning in, I begin to read. I don't worry about tripping over words for once, because I know this important scene by heart and the illustrations help to guide me.

"Unbelievable," Bes says, kicking a wall. "Lumped together with an asrai and a hobgoblin. I fight only with my sisters. Not with pretty things. Hairy things."

Wilf guffaws. "Eh? Hairy things, you say? That's rich! So it's bad to be hairy, but feathers are all right. I mean, turning into a bird. *Oh, no. That's not weird at all.*"

In the drawings, Kit has been sitting back, ignoring their argument and eating an apple, contemplating their situation. Now he speaks up.

"The Ravens will wait to attack. They always seem to wait until you're up high, close to a bell itself. Gives them the advantage."

"Makes sense, I s'pose," Wilf replies. "Let us expend the energy. The higher we go, the harder we fall when they pluck us out of a belfry and dump us outside."

"Speak for yourself." Bes stretches her arms out to look like wings. "*I'm* not falling anywhere."

"Still going on about feathers," Wilf says. "What's *your* brilliant plan then, bird girl?"

"Maybe thinking like them – like a bird. You know, having me here is an advantage for you. Did you ever stop to think for a moment that it might be useful having a bird around?"

"No. Too much getting up at dawn. Too much cheeping. *Cheep, cheep, cheep.*"

Out of nowhere, Kit's apple core flies at the pair, bouncing off Bes's head and hitting Wilf's before falling to the floor.

Mouths open, the pair look over at him.

"I've just had an idea. And maybe, if we're lucky, it'll work," he says.

That's when they figure out how they can use Bes's powers to help them all fly.

With a smile on my face, I continue. I enter the room closest to me and move silently along the length of the large, scrawled-upon wall. Every inch is taken up with scene after scene. They are all here. All of them. You could read the books right off the walls. I keep going. Faster. I dodge two ladders and start up the stairs. Everywhere, all around me – high and low – is the story I know so well.

I pause at my favourite parts. The funny parts. The sad parts. And then, of course, there are the parts where Edie St Clair reached in, took my heart right out of my chest, slammed it to the floor, and jumped up and down on it. I can't help but stop at those parts.

When fighting, the Ravens wear silver spurs attached to their legs. During a raid in book four, Bes's older sister Ash is pierced by a Raven spur. It isn't until Kit, Wilf and Bes, along with Bes's other sister Marlie, retreat to the hideaway that they realise the extent of Ash's injuries.

Ash dies, her blood staining the floor in a large pool. Over the coming days, weeks, months, Bes refuses to clean it away. She argues about it with Wilf one time when she catches him trying to cover the stain with an old rug.

"Eh, it's not healthy, girl," he says. "You're obsessed with that mark. Always staring at it."

Bes throws herself across the room at him.

"Never cover that stain," Bes tells him, grabbing his dirty shirt and pulling him towards her. "Do you hear me? Never. Don't you understand? I need to see it. I need to see it every single day until the last Raven is defeated. I need to remember what it is I'm fighting for."

Two books later, Bes loses her other sister in a different raid – her precious younger sister, Marlie. In order to get away with their own lives, Kit, Wilf and Bes have to leave Marlie's broken body behind, atop a church spire. Bes is hysterical. Kit and Wilf have to lock her up overnight so she won't go back for Marlie's body and be killed herself. But then Marlie's body is miraculously delivered to them via a raft on the Thames. Kit and Wilf are worried it's a trap, of course. But it turns out that it's not a trap at all, and Bes is reunited with her sister's body.

This tells them there must be a Raven who is sympathetic to their cause – a Raven who might just be willing to help them. The reader doesn't find out who is actually behind this act of kindness until the next book.

I hesitate before taking a step towards the wall this scene lies on, reluctant to live this moment over again.

My fingers reach out to touch the drawing of Marlie on the raft, the great swirling Thames surrounding her. She is cocooned by white roses. Safe now. Safe with Ash.

Readers had burned copies of the book after discovering that Edie St Clair had killed Marlie. They'd vowed never to read another of her books, or see another of her movies. They'd sent her horrible messages and spray-painted the pavement in front of her house.

Edie St Clair sighs. "I actually didn't know I was going to do it until it happened. I hated doing it. But it had to be done."

"But why *Bes*? Why does she need to suffer so much?" Even as I ask the question, I think I know the answer.

"Because she's the hardest one to break."

It's true. Painful, but true. "Still, it's not fair."

"I never said it was fair."

I turn back to the wall and begin to read.

"They've taken everything from me now," Bes sobs, cradling Marlie to her. Kit kneels behind her, his hands on her shoulders, while Wilf stands guard, watching the skies.

"Not everything," Kit replies after some time. "Not quite."

"Eh, that's right. And the little that's left . . . ?" Wilf waits for the other two to look up at him. "Now we take that back."

I stand and stare at this scene for some time before I move on, Edie St Clair silent behind me.

For hours, I let the drawings lead me on, my eyes skimming the walls.

Book seven.

Book eight.

Book nine.

As book nine finishes, I pause. I am on the top floor of the townhouse. I look at the drawings that continue along the pale white walls beyond.

The End.

I'm reading what no other reader has been allowed to set eyes on.

Am I allowed to go on? I look back at Edie St Clair, who is still following me.

"It's all right," Edie St Clair says, urging me on. "You need to keep going. To understand."

I keep going down the corridor. There is an open door to my right and another, down the corridor, which is closed. That one catches my attention. It's the only one in this townhouse that is firmly shut.

"Not that door," Edie St Clair says quickly.

I glance at her and she looks away.

This only makes me more curious. What's behind it?

But there's no time for questions. Edie St Clair ushers me through the open door to my right. Again, there is no furniture, only bare floorboards. The difference here is that the room is only half-filled with drawings – two walls are glaringly bare. My fingers run over the drawings as I read. I cheer at the victories, gasp as I see what's in store for my friends and wonder how the ending will play out. It's got to be the battle. Everyone's been waiting for the faeries to finally storm the White Tower – the old keep at the Tower of London, which the Ravens have turned into their stronghold. Everyone's been anxious to see how Edie St Clair will pull this off with the faerie numbers so low.

But no one storms the White Tower. Instead, the story takes a strange turn, going around and around in circles. Nothing is happening. It's like everything was leading up to the final battle and then . . . well, the story has come to a standstill. Something is wrong.

My outstretched hand falters.

Edie St Clair comes to stand beside me. "Do you understand now? Why I can't finish?"

"I . . ."

"Don't you see? It's not me. It's *them*. They won't let me finish. They won't let me write the final scenes."

"They?" Who is she talking about? Her fans?

She moves to the wall. "Look, here." She taps one spot, grubby and scribbled upon. "I've almost drawn myself in several times to see if I can sort it out with them. But I'm scared of what might happen. I don't trust my characters any more. They're angry with me."

Um, what? She can't possibly mean . . .

"Yes, it's true, Tamsin. I've gone in there before. Into their world. The London of the Bells. You've got to understand. These characters of mine are so real to so many people – so important. Being so loved by so many has given them . . . life, I suppose you'd call it. A kind of life. A life apart from me. That and the world I've created on these walls has given me the ability to draw myself into their world. To enter it whenever I want to. And I need to do that again now, to work this out. I've never told anyone else I can do this, but I need you to know where I've gone in case something happens to me while I'm in there."

I begin to move away from her. She hasn't told anyone about this? Then why me? Why now?

"Wait," she says, her voice echoing in the empty space. "Tamsin, please . . . I need you to understand. I need your help."

I can only stare at her in horror. At thin, sick Edie St Clair.

Because now I do understand.

I understand that Edie St Clair doesn't just have an insane townhouse.

Edie St Clair is insane.

I run home. I run down the stairs to our basement apartment. I run away from Edie St Clair. I run away from the world.

I don't go to the private park.

I don't go to Edie St Clair's house.

In my room, I surround myself with my drawings. I drown myself in them. I draw Kit, Wilf and Bes. I draw the bell towers. I draw the world I feel more comfortable in than this one. I barely look up as my pen flies over page after page. I've got to keep drawing. Keeping on drawing means I don't have to think.

I don't have to think about Edie St Clair's words.

I don't have to think about Edie St Clair.

But I *do* think about her.

I can't stop.

Why can't she be normal? Why can't she go back to her normal house with its normal study and draw with me? Draw that final battle scene that everyone wants? Finish her book that everyone is waiting for? I don't want her telling me ridiculous things. I don't want her saying she can draw herself into her stories. I hate her.

Hate.

Her.

Ugh, I've wrecked my drawing now. My lines are too thick. Too harsh. Too angry. Frustrated, I scribble all over it.

I was stupid.

Stupid to think I was special. That she wanted to draw with me.

I was nothing but a distraction. Something to take her mind off what she was supposed to be doing.

She'll never finish that dumb book.

One day later . . .

I'm sitting at my desk. I've been busy all day reading a graphic novel that isn't Edie St Clair's, and not drawing her characters.

"Hey, kid."

It's the journalist.

"You seen Edie St Clair today?"

I shake my head.

"You know she's missing, right?"

It's true.

Edie St Clair is missing.

Edie St Clair had an important appointment she didn't show up for. Her brother hasn't heard from her. Her agent says she should be at home. Her housekeeper says that she didn't mention anything about going away. Her phone is turned off.

Edie St Clair's brother is very worried.

Edie St Clair's agent is very worried.

Edie St Clair's housekeeper is very worried.

And now the police are worried, too. They think she might have been kidnapped.

A police officer comes to speak to me. She knew that I had been drawing with Edie St Clair. I told her that I had stopped. She asked me why and I told her it was because Edie St Clair was sick. I considered telling the police officer what Edie had told me – about her characters – but she was called away to help deal with the journalists. There are more of them now than ever before.

I don't want to go outside among the media. But I'm also curious. Where's Edie St Clair?

I creep outside. Make my way up one stone step after another. Looking. Listening.

Until I'm spotted.

"Ah, there you are!" the journalist says. "Tell me about your famous friend. How long has it been since you've seen her? Did she say anything? Anything at all?"

"Hey, you. Back off!" a police officer says. It's the one from the park. "You must be Tamsin. The housekeeper was wanting to talk to you. Come with me."

He opens the iron gate. Before I can protest, he takes

my arm. Pushes past the journalists. Leads me up to the front door. Rings the bell.

Mrs Marchant answers. "Tamsin. Oh, good. Do come in. I've just put the kettle on."

Mrs Marchant takes me into the kitchen. She gives me tea and biscuits. She asks me all the same questions the police officer asked me.

Did you see Edie this morning?

No.

You're sure you didn't see her leave the house?

No. I mean, yes, I'm sure.

Were you supposed to come and draw this afternoon?

Um, we hadn't made plans.

Mrs Marchant's hands flutter, picking up and putting down two small cardboard boxes that lie on the spotless glass table. "Her medication," she tells me, when she sees me looking. "She's on two different types of antibiotics for pneumonia and she's not taken them with her. What if she gets worse? Oh, I just don't understand it. She always tells me where she's going. And her book is due in just a few days' time. This isn't like her. She was trying to finish it before the deadline. I actually thought she might."

Mrs Marchant makes me eat a biscuit. As I sit, my gaze flicks down the hallway to that other door. The one that leads into the second, empty, townhouse.

It's ajar.

So, Mrs Marchant knows about the townhouse. But

is that all she knows? Edie St Clair said she hadn't told anyone else about drawing herself into the London of the Bells.

Mrs Marchant sees me looking at the door. She sighs. "The police have been in there, of course. They've searched it. Top to bottom."

I stare at her. She doesn't seem to think it's strange that Edie has a townhouse just so she can draw on the walls. But then I remember the owners of the townhouse I live in. I can't remember them ever even visiting, let alone drawing on the walls.

"Oh, but I'm so worried about her. I just don't know where she could have got to."

I continue to say nothing and nibble on my biscuit. I feel something warm and furry brush up against my leg.

"Ink!" I reach down.

"Oh, I wouldn't . . ."

I rub Ink's head like I'd done last time. "It's okay. He likes me." I pick Ink up and put him on my lap. He purrs contentedly.

"Goodness!" Mrs Marchant's eyes are wide. "You *are* special!"

The doorbell startles all three of us, and Ink jumps off my lap.

"I'd best get that." Mrs Marchant rises. I watch her lemon-coloured cardigan bob down the grey hall.

I stare at the door, still ajar.

I make sure Mrs Marchant is busy.

And then I slip out of my seat.

I might not have seen Edie St Clair, but I know where to look for her.

I don't pause to look around the townhouse. I run as softly as I can over to the stairs. I keep running. Up and up. Up to the top floor. All the time wondering . . .

Could it be true?

No.

Of course not.

Of course not.

Don't be ridiculous.

I stop in the doorway. My eyes move to the space that has been crossed out. Rubbed out. Fought over.

Below that space is a pen. A thick black pen, lying on the floor.

A lid lies next to it.

Slowly, I walk over to the wall.

It takes me only seconds to find what I'm looking for.

There it is.

She is.

There is a new drawing. It is of Edie St Clair. I recognise her short, dark bob. Her boots.

Can it really be true? I'd thought she was crazy. But there she is, on the wall, while she's missing in the real world.

Without taking my eyes off her, I bend down and pick up the pen.

I draw myself on the blank wall.

And everything turns black.

I'M on my back, my arms by my sides, my fingers splayed out against a rough wooden floor. But as my eyes flicker open, I see it's not the floor of the room I was just in. The ceiling is too high, and dusty wooden beams hang heavy above.

I try to push myself up, but my head spins. I lie back down and let my eyes explore instead.

Light streams through some wooden shutters, particles of dust spinning through the air.

I turn my head and see gigantic bronze bells hanging in the shadows.

Twelve of them.

I blink, and when I focus again, the bells are still there. Bells with – I force myself to get up now, not caring if I feel dizzy – bells with words scrawled all over them.

I race over to one of the shutters, but they're stuck tight with age. The next shutter over, however, has a broken slat. I bend down and peer through the gap.

I'm met with a view of a crumbling London. A mix of broken glass and thatch, Tudor-black wood and warped steel. The old maintained, the new left to rot and wear. This is the way the Ravens like things.

I stare for I don't know how long.

I can't believe it.

I'm in the London of the Bells. I'm in a belfry in the London of the Bells.

It worked. It actually worked.

Which means Edie is in here, too. Somewhere.

"Edie," I whisper.

No answer.

A little louder. "*Edie.*"

Still nothing.

Quietly, cautiously, I cross the creaky wooden boards to read the words etched onto the closest bell. These words are how the Ravens control London. The bells are scattered throughout the city, and the words have been scratched on them by the Ravens' cruel beaks. Once a command is inscribed, the bells can be activated in two different ways. Either a Raven taps its beak upon the bell itself, or the beak that traced the words speaks the phrase from afar and taps three times upon any iron surface.

When this bell rings, Sector 32 will sleep.

When this bell rings, Sector 24 will work.

When this bell rings, Sector 26 will eat.

Once the inscription is activated, it will begin to light up, one letter at a time. The bell will chime. And any Londoners within hearing will be forced through stolen faerie magic to do the Ravens' bidding. This is how London continues to be stupefied by the constant ringing of the twelve bells, its life and soul sucked away. It's only London that's affected. A magical wall on the city's outskirts makes sure of that. And the rest of the world? Well, the Ravens don't care about anywhere else. London *is* the world for them. No other place matters.

The only group not affected by the Ravens' abuse of the bells are those who are half faerie and half human, like Kit, Wilf and Bes. It was some time before the faerie folk and humankind bred, breaking the taboo. There were so few of these children, and they were so young . . . the Ravens hadn't considered them a threat.

I reach out to touch the dusty wooden beam beside me. It's strange, but it feels more real to me than anything at home. Everything seems more real here, despite the fact that the London of the Bells looks like medieval London. This is the world of my heart. Horses and carts, cobblestones and watercress, nonsense and nursery rhymes. The Ravens *adore* nursery rhymes. My eyes on the bell, I sing under my breath.

Oranges and lemons, say the bells of St Clement's.
Bull's eyes and targets, say the bells of St Margaret's.
Brickbats and tiles, say the bells of St Giles'.
Halfpence and farthings, say the bells of St Martin's.
Pancakes and fritters, say the bells of St Peter's.

Two sticks and an apple, say the bells of Whitechapel.
Maids in white aprons, say the bells of St Katherine's.
Pokers and tongs, say the bells of St John's.
Kettles and pans, say the bells of St Anne's.
Old Father Baldpate, say the slow bells of Aldgate.
You owe me ten shillings, say the bells of St Helen's.
When will you pay me, say the bells of Old Bailey.
When I grow rich, say the bells of Shoreditch.
Pray, when will that be? Say the bells of Stepney.
I do not know, says the great bell of Bowe.

The bells don't say these things any more. Instead, they sing a dull song of the Ravens' orders.

I whisper the final two lines of the rhyme.

Here comes the candle to light you to bed.

And here comes the chopper to chop off your head.

This is what the Ravens swear they'll do to Kit, Wilf and Bes. When they finally catch them, they'll chop off their heads at the Tower of London – the Ravens' base.

A hissing noise startles me. It's coming from a bell on my far left. I run over to look at it and see an inscription begin to light up.

When this bell rings, you will seek out the intruder in our midst.

It takes a moment or two for the words to sink in. *The intruder in our midst.*

Wait.

Me?

I'm the intruder?

It must mean me. But how did they know I was coming? The hissing sound continues, slow and steady.

What should I do? What if this is real? What if I'm not safe here?

I've got to run. I've got to hide.

I look around the room, searching for an escape route.

There, in the corner. I spot some stairs, leading down.

I bolt towards them, throwing myself down the stone steps as fast as I can. I'm sure I hear a beating of wings against the shutters as I go, but I don't look back to check. I don't dare. The stairs circle around and around, seeming to go on forever. Around and around and around. I take one turn too wide and scrape my elbow on something sharp sticking out from the wall. The graze immediately begins to burn and blood oozes from the wound. I move faster as I realise what this means. This is no dream. I'm *not* safe. I have to get out of here.

Just when I think the stairs will never end, they do, and I burst through a small wooden door. I trip over an iron boot scraper and stumble into the dirty street. A horse and cart passes by, loaded with wood, while another follows it, stacked with bread. A large group of men in tattered clothes pass by in formation. The men hear the thump of the door and turn to look at me, but their glazed eyes show no interest. I am merely an obstacle. The bells have instructed them to do one task and one task only, and that task does not involve seeing me.

I have to keep moving. I have to find somewhere to hide. I know that when the bell rings, the words upon it will register deep within them, and their eyes will turn hungry.

I hurl myself out onto the cobbled street before them.

They continue to look at me blankly, but go on their way.

I dodge them and stick to the side of the street, listening for the flap of wings that's surely coming. I run past shop after shop. There's a bank, a supermarket, a sandwich shop, all their signage worn or falling off. With no electricity, the doors are shut tight. There's nowhere for me to hide.

Then I see it – a recessed entry to a disused office building. I duck behind one of its wide pillars, then scan the empty street, trying to work out what to do next.

Something above my head catches my eye – an Underground sign. The station is Bank.

Wait. I know where I am.

I'm in Cheapside.

I'm in Cheapside, and that was the belfry of St Mary le Bow – the great bell of Bowe.

My head whips back around and I take in the streetscape again, barely believing my eyes. In my world, this space would be busy. Red double-decker buses would fly past. The office glass would gleam. People would scurry by seeking sandwiches, coffee, running to meetings. But not here. Not in this broken world.

I jump as the bell finally begins to peal, the sound bouncing off the smashed glass of the buildings, filling the potholed, rubbish-filled street.

As I'm trying to figure out what to do next, I hear the *clip-clop* of horses' hooves underneath the ringing sound. A horse and cart turns out of a side street. The driver's eyes are everywhere. I slide back behind the pillar before he sees me.

Where am I going to go?

I need to find Kit and Wilf and Bes. I need to find my friends. They'll know what to do.

I listen carefully. When I'm sure the horse and cart has gone, I peer out again.

Oh, no.

The group of men I saw before has turned around and is heading my way. They've broken off into small groups, and their eyes are no longer blank. They're bright and hungry as they search doorways and entrances. They look high and low.

They are hunting for me.

The intruder.

Which means I have to hide properly.

Now.

There are four more pillars running along the outside of the building. I bolt from one to the next. There aren't many choices from here. It's either out into the street, or behind me, into the Underground, which isn't a safe place in this London, the London of the Bells. It seems like the obvious choice, because the Ravens won't go there – it's too easy for them to become trapped, unable to fly away. The problem is that the Underground is the domain of the faeries, and not all faeries are good.

I'll have to take my chances on the street. I just need to make it out of earshot of the bell, into a sector that's busy with everyday chores.

But how am I going to stay out of sight?

I look up the street. Further along is a ghostly white, dirt-streaked Victorian building of Portland stone with plenty of alcoves to hide in. I check both ways. The direction the building is in is clear. The group of men I'd passed before are still advancing from the other way.

I make a break for it.

I sprint away from the last pillar, my eyes focused on the building ahead.

But there's a problem.

I hadn't counted on the small laneway to my right.

Halfway along it, there's a group of men and women. Like the other group, they are checking in doorways and stairwells. Anywhere I could possibly be.

In the middle of the street, I freeze.

As the people in the group spot me, their eyes light up. They know I'm the intruder they've been called to find. Everything about me is wrong. My clothes. My movements. The fact that I am by myself.

Their mouths open as one. The bell still pealing high overhead, they begin to croak in the language of the Ravens. The deep, throaty rattle reverberates in the street, building higher and higher.

Kraah-kraah, kraah-kraah-kraah.

Kraah-kraah, kraah-kraah-kraah.

They start towards me in a pack.

I have to keep going. I have to run. Away from the sound of the bell. Away from the Ravens.

But before I can move, someone grabs me from behind. More than one person. A hand goes over my mouth. Another over my eyes.

I struggle. Kick. Flail.

But it's no good.

Quickly, efficiently, I am dragged backwards into the deep, dark Underground.

SOMEONE kicks my feet out from under me and I'm lifted up. Whoever is carrying me is running, my body jolting. I have to escape. I writhe and bite the hand that's covering my mouth. It pushes down on my face harder, making it difficult to breathe.

The jolting gets worse as we go down. Down, down, down. I realise it must be one of the old, steep escalators. We're going down into the depths of the city, where no Raven would dare go, lest its wings never find the freedom of the sky again. I struggle even harder as I realise how isolated I'll be down here. Anything could happen to me in the Underground, and no one in the real world would ever know.

I'd just be gone – like Edie.

I think about what that would mean. My mother left all alone in our tiny apartment, the cold, silent house looming above. My desk empty at school.

But, no. I can't give up hope so easily. Kit, Wilf and Bes wouldn't. I have to fight back like they would.

There is the creak of metal, then I'm thrown onto a cold tiled floor, my mouth and eyes released.

It is pitch black.

"What did you want to go and bite me for?" a voice says. "What sort of thanks is that for saving you?"

A match strikes, a candle is lit, and I finally see my captors.

It's *them*.

I'm actually in the same room as them. And my eyes are open. I'm not just conjuring them up, like I do in my bedroom.

The threesome stand above me. Wilf round and scrappy, his beanie pushed back on his head. Bes, frowning as she ignores me and inspects her bitten hand. Kit, tall, white-blond and angular, with crossed arms and that constant half-grin of his. They're really here. Moving. Colourful and alive. So much more alive than in my drawings.

I make a strange noise as I suck in some air and scramble backwards, hitting a desk. Old, yellowed papers fall onto the floor.

"Eh, what's this?" Wilf says, looking over at Kit. "It's her. But not."

"Her who?" Bes finally looks up from her wound to take me in properly. She does a double take and then lunges forward to grab me by my T-shirt, her muscular arms jerking me upright. "What are you doing here? You think that after all we've been through you can just—"

"Bes! Stop!" Kit pulls her off me. She kicks out at him as he grabs her arms and wrestles her across to the far side of the room.

"I . . ." I'm left gasping. I stumble back and hit the wall. Why would Bes attack me? I always thought that if we met she'd really see me. Understand me. I thought we'd be instant friends.

Bes continues to struggle, making strange bird-like shrieks as Kit pins her to the wall.

She's crazed.

Wilf goes over to help him and receives a kick in the leg for it. "Eh, cut it out! Keep your feathers in place."

"Look. We don't know why she's here," Kit says. "Just settle down while we figure this out."

After some more angry thrashing, Bes begins to calm down. All I can think is that she's angry because I'm from the real world. I'm not supposed to be here. I'm as much an intruder to them as I am to the Ravens.

The threesome huddle together.

"I don't like it. It's weird," Wilf says.

"It has to mean something," Kit replies.

"But what?" Bes glares.

The three of them turn to stare at me.

In the silence, I say the first thing that comes to my addled mind. "I can't believe that I . . . I mean . . . you're . . . you're not real."

"Eh, that's great. That's just charming." Wilf spits.

"The 'you're nothing but a fictional character' bit, right out of the gate! Not into pleasantries, this one!"

"I'm sorry! I didn't mean that. You're as real as anything to me. Of course you are. I draw you all the time."

"You draw us all the time." Wilf snorts. "Really."

But Kit holds out a hand to silence him. "Wait. Explain yourself," he says.

I pause for a moment or two, not wanting to say anything stupid again. "Well, I mean . . . I've always drawn you. I've always loved Edie St Clair's books. She lives next door to me. We've been drawing together lately. She showed me how she can draw herself into her books. Then she disappeared, so I've come to find her so she can finish her final book. Have you seen her? Do you know where she is? She's not well. She needs to get home and keep taking her medication."

Silence.

The three of them exchange glances.

Finally, Bes goes to move forward. Kit puts out a hand to stop her, but she shakes it off. "It's okay," she says.

She doesn't look angry, not like before. Just the same, I find myself pushing back into the wall.

"You're saying you've come to find Edie St Clair, so she can finish her final book," she repeats, her dark eyes staring at me as if I'm crazy.

Maybe I am crazy. I don't know. Either way, I nod.

She continues to inspect me for a moment or two, then she turns and zips back to the others.

They huddle together again. This time all I hear is murmuring.

That is, until all three of them jolt at the same time and look upwards.

"What is it?" I say.

"You can't hear that?" Bes says. "It's a bell."

"Of course I can't hear it. I'm not faerie. I'm not even half faerie."

"But you're . . ." Wilf starts.

Kit gives him a shove. "Don't! She doesn't know. She said she came to find Edie St Clair. Think about it. She must be here for a reason. Maybe it'll work in our favour if we play along?"

"What are you talking about?" I look from Kit to Wilf. "What's going on?"

"We can argue about it later," Bes chirrups. "Right now we have to go to St Dunstan's. We can't waste any more time. That was a destruction chime."

"Oh, no!" I cry. A destruction chime means a group of Londoners are about to be destroyed. The Ravens collect the unwanted Londoners into one sector, close to the Thames, and then have the bells bid them walk straight into the river.

One step after another they go, unable to stop themselves. The faerie folk despise seeing their magic abused in this way. Especially because a destruction chime often targets the weak – small children, sick people, old people. The Ravens, knowing how the faeries are repulsed by such suffering, often use a destruction chime as a trap, trying to flush the faerie folk out from underground and eliminate them.

Bes is already at the door. "Come on, you two."

"We can't leave her here," Kit says. "What if something happens to her? You don't know what that might mean for us."

"What? You want to take her too? Oh, great. More hangers on. Literally. You honestly expect me to fly with all three of you? *And* outrun any Ravens we come across?"

"You can do it," Kit says.

Wilf shakes his head. "Nah, you've got to tell her she *can't* do it. That's how this one operates."

"Didn't say I *couldn't* do it. Only that I don't *want* to."

"See?" Wilf laughs. "Told you so."

Bes tweets an ear-piercing sound that is directed at me. "Ugh. You'd better hang on tight. If you fall, I'm not turning back."

I'M flying.

I'm actually flying.

The sky is clear, the breeze is in my face. My body trembles with a strange mix of wonder and terror as the wind rushes past. I look down in awe at laneways and buildings, trees and apartments, mosques and hospitals, and the long, grey ribbon of the Thames to our right.

Once we'd climbed to the top of the station escalators, Kit, Wilf and Bes regrouped. Kit ran on ahead and checked outside. He said there were several groups on the street, but no one immediately outside the entrance to the station. He couldn't see any Ravens. Wilf and Bes guessed there might be some around, but that most of them would be in Stepney, dealing with the destruction chime at St Dunstan's.

That's where the danger would be.

"Do we need to go through the plan?" Kit said.

"I think we've got it down by now," Bes replied. "Get as close as we can to the bell. Immobilise it. Don't get killed."

"The not getting killed part is always my favourite bit," Wilf said.

"Don't forget we'll be near the Tower," Kit reminded everyone. "We'll need to be extra careful."

The Tower. There had always been Ravens at the Tower of London because of a long-held superstition. If its six captive Ravens left the Tower, it was believed that the Crown would fall, and Britain with it.

No one had ever dreamed it would be the ravens who remained and the Crown who fled.

The King and his family had escaped at the last possible moment – just before the bells had first struck their magical chimes and that invisible barrier had been drawn around the outskirts of London. While Britain hadn't fallen, it *had* lost its capital. That was over ten years ago now. Ten years of London suffering under the rule of the Ravens and their bells.

"And what am I supposed to do with this?" Bes jerked a thumb at me.

"Stick her somewhere safe, I guess?" Wilf said. "Reckon she can get hurt?"

"I cut myself before." I held out my grazed elbow. "Here. In this world."

"There's our answer," Kit said.

I watched as Kit unwound a thin strip of tan leather from his wrists. I'd seen him do this so many times in the graphic novels, and in the movies. I held my breath, waiting to see it happen for real.

A rustling noise and a puff of air made me look back over at Bes.

Except she wasn't there.

Wilf looked up and around the inside of the disused station, his eyes coming to rest on a metal beam. "Spotted!"

Before I could find her, Bes swooped past my head and came to perch upon Wilf's shoulder.

In sand martin form, Bes was smaller than my hand. She was delicate and fragile, with a creamy beige breast, the most perfectly pointed angular wings and a tiny triangle of a beak.

As she stared in my direction, I realised I'd never had a bird look at me with such loathing before.

I still couldn't understand why she hated me. And it wasn't anything I'd said, because it had been from the moment she'd taken a proper look at me.

That expression of loathing reminded me of the very first time Bes had come to rest upon Wilf. Edie St Clair had captured it perfectly in one of her illustrations. It had been after that raid on St Leonard's – that first time they'd flown together. Bes had been in sand martin form and Wilf had held out an arm for her to set down upon. She'd circled him, given him the exact look I'd just received, and finally settled on his shoulder. And then she'd reached her tiny beak over and plucked a hair out of his ear. After returning to bodily form, the loathing had remained in Bes's human eyes.

"When I want to sit on your ugly green arm, I'll tell you," she'd said.

Maybe that's it, I'd thought. It was about trust. Maybe she thought she'd saved a Londoner when she'd dragged me off the street, but then realised I was actually from the real world. Maybe she just didn't trust me yet. Well, I'd show her. I'd earn her trust.

Bes hovered over each of us in turn, flapping her wings and releasing the dust that would help us fly.

And then I saw what I'd been waiting for – Kit tied the tiny strip of leather to one of her feet.

"Whatever you do, don't let go," he told me, passing the leather strip over. "She was probably serious about not turning back for you."

With a gulp, I wound the strap carefully around my hand like I'd seen the others do, and let Kit check my grip.

Now, in the sky, I'm holding on so tight that my knuckles are white. For a moment, I close my eyes – not out of fear, but because it's still so hard to believe that I'm here. Here in the London of the Bells. Exactly where I've always dreamed of being. When I open my eyes again, I look up ahead of me at Kit, his tunic flapping in the wind. Then behind me, at Wilf, his eyes shut tight. (He's always hated flying.) And I grin a silly, wide grin.

How this is possible, I don't know. All I know is that it's not a dream.

I'm here.

I'm really here.

I'm *home*.

Home. The word makes me pause. It seems strange to call this my home, but that's what it feels like. I belong here. I don't belong in the real world, where people make fun of my reading and spelling. Where people think I'm stupid. I spread my fingers wide and try to catch the air that flows through them. And I grin again. *Home*.

I begin to hear the clear chime of a bell. Faint at first, and then louder as we close in on the church. We dip down lower, and Bes drops us onto the roof of a long row of terrace houses. Kit unties the leather strap from Bes's tiny leg.

"Be careful!" Wilf calls, but she's already gone, darting and swooping to the right, off to see what's going on.

Wilf and Kit give each other worried looks. I can see the problem. Bes will be easily spotted – sand martins shouldn't be here, in the city. They belong on salt-encrusted sea cliffs. Also, in the London of the Bells, the Ravens have frightened all the other birds away. Bes will have to use her size, speed and wits to her advantage.

The three of us stare blankly into the distance, waiting for a glimpse of Bes. The bell fills the silence that lies heavy between us. It's less than a minute before Bes returns. She lands on the wedge of rooftop we're standing on and, with a flutter of her outstretched wings, rises into bodily form, her feathers seemingly melting away as she stretches and takes shape. I watch, amazed. I've seen her make the transformation in Edie's black and white drawings, and watched an actor do this in the movies, care of technology, but to see it happen right in front of me . . .

"What are you gawping at?" she barks at me.

"Sorry," I mumble.

She turns to the others. "They're walking a large group towards the Thames. They're not far off, but we've got a bit of time. The problem is, it's St Dunstan's. You know the issues here."

"Out in the open," Wilf says.

"Poor access," Kit adds.

"It'll have to be me," Bes says. "So don't argue about it."

"She's right," Wilf says.

"I'm always right."

"Yeah. So you're always telling us."

Kit doesn't look happy, but he doesn't argue. "I'll make my way down to the river. If the Ravens get everyone that far, I can save the Londoners from there."

Being half asrai, Kit is unstoppable in the water. It helps that the Ravens fear the river with its strong currents.

A second bell begins to chime, blending in with the first. The three of them sigh simultaneously.

"And there's the bell for us," Bes says. "I was wondering when they'd get around to that."

Wilf snorts. "Eh, be fair. They're busy birds. Dust baths to roll in, seed to peck at, major cities to destroy . . ."

"This sector – fifty-eight – has been instructed to capture us. Alive," Kit tells me. "But that's only so the Ravens can have the pleasure of chopping off our heads later."

I wince.

"Are we going to get on with this, or just stand around chatting all day?" Bes says.

"Chatting works for me," Wilf replies. "Maybe we can find a couple of deck chairs somewhere. Pick out a spot in the sun. Work on our tans. Wait. Can green skin tan?"

"Hilarious. You head for the river." Bes points to Kit. "I'll drop these two closer. *She'll* want to watch, I suppose. I'll find them a safe position, do another pass to see what's going on, and then come back for Wilf when the time's right."

"Do I get any say in this?" Wilf asks.

"No," Kit and Bes say at the same time.

"Right, then." Wilf rubs his hands together. "Sounds like one of our usual plans. Let's go."

Once again, Bes changes form and showers us with dust. Kit ties the leather strap to her leg. This time, however, it's only Wilf and myself that hold onto it.

"See you soon!" Kit bounds off along the row of rooftops.

Be careful, Kit, I think as I watch him leave.

Please, be careful.

WE don't fly for long this time. Bes soon sets us down on another set of terraced rooftops. She doesn't change back into her bodily form, but settles and lets Wilf untie the thin leather strap. He winds the strap around his arm, tucking the end into itself for safekeeping.

His expression is as dark as a Raven's wing. "Don't be long or I'll start to miss your ugly mug."

Bes settles on his shoulder for a moment, chirrups a reply and is gone. Wilf tracks her until she's out of sight. Even then, his eyes remain fixed on the place she was last visible.

The bells continue to clang their ugly message of hate.

"Um, shouldn't we hide?" I say.

"What?" Wilf looks over at me, as if he's completely forgotten I was here at all. "Oh. Yeah. Guess so. Cop a squat over there, why don't you?"

I perch next to a chimney that's in the shade of a higher rooftop. A tree in front provides some cover. I shouldn't be noticed here, but I can still see the church's bell tower quite well. The space we have is small, but Wilf still makes a point to sit as far away from me as is humanly (or hobgoblinly) possible, without being seen. Again, I feel the sting of being disliked. I still can't believe how Bes attacked me back in the Underground. I can't forget her ferocious expression – how she'd launched at me like an animal. She really wanted to hurt me. She would have, too, if Kit hadn't pulled her off. I want to ask Wilf why she acted that way, but I also don't want to talk about it. I'd been so excited to meet Bes, only to find she wants nothing to do with me. So I continue to sit next to Wilf in cold silence. There is no movement in the sky. No Ravens. No Bes.

A few minutes later, another kind of movement catches my attention. I turn my head quickly to the left. Was it my imagination, or did Wilf just shuffle closer towards me?

He clears his throat, but says nothing.

Maybe it *was* my imagination?

My attention moves back to the sky.

Shuffle, shuffle.

Okay, it's not my imagination.

I watch as Wilf removes his beanie. Fiddles with it. "So, um . . ."

I wait.

"Yeah, so . . . I'm more than just my stomach, you know," he says.

We both look at his stomach. There's a lot of it hanging over his belt.

"Sure, it takes up about ninety per cent of my body, but I'm not just about the tea and biscuits. Or the jokes. There's more to me than food and laughs. There are feelings under all the wobbly bits, eh? Anyway . . . just wanted to get all that out in the open. Have my say, like."

What is he going on about?

I take a moment to look at him. Really look at him. Not at his stout, hairy body, his grimy, greenish skin, his grubby nails and dirty beanie. I look past these things. "I know that," I finally say. "Everyone knows that."

He looks surprised. "They do?"

"Yes. Of course. You don't think everyone loves you because you're funny, do you? Or because you're always yabbering on about your next meal?"

He shrugs. "Dunno what I think."

It's my turn to shuffle sideways. I edge closer to him and look deep into his eyes. "Wilf, readers don't love you because you make them laugh. They love you for the same reason Kit and Bes love you. Because you're *loyal*. Loyal and true and trustworthy, and so many other amazing things."

He stares at me for some time before he replies. "Huh. Loyal and true and trustworthy, you reckon?"

"Yes."

"Didn't know that."

I feel a pang that he would think people believe he's

shallow. That he's a character who is included just for laughs. It's not true at all. At least, that's how I feel as a reader. I'm sure Edie St Clair thinks the same.

We both look out at the sky again.

Shuffle, shuffle.

"So, er, what happens after all this?"

I'm surprised to see how close he is to me now. We're almost touching.

"What happens after this raid, you mean?"

"Nah, after all this . . ." He sweeps an arm.

"Oh." He means after the series. After the last book.

"Reckon there might be someone for me?"

I blink.

"Kit had that whatever-you-call-it with the tree sprite. Bes has that love-hate thing with that troll. Even most of the Ravens have someone, don't they? It would be all right. If I had someone, too. Hobgoblin, human, I'm not picky. Maybe that tree sprite of Kit's has a friend. She was a looker, that tree sprite, wasn't she?" He nudges me with his elbow. "So, um, what do you reckon?"

It takes me a moment to recall his actual question. "I think it's possible. And they'd be lucky to have you – tree sprite, hobgoblin, human, whoever."

"Yeah? Well, that's good to know. If you could . . ." He stops himself.

"If I could what?"

"Eh, nothing."

"Really. You can tell me."

"Nah, I wanted to ask is all. See what you thought." He looks at my arm and his – so close together – and then shuffles the other way along the rooftop. "Probably shouldn't have mentioned it."

I hold out a hand. I don't want to lose him now. His talk gave me hope. Wilf didn't hate me. Maybe Bes would come around as well?

"I can ask Edie for you. When I find her."

"Yeah, I guess." His eyes are fixed back on the bell tower. Our talk is over. "Where's Bes? She shouldn't be taking so long. Eh, I don't like this. Doesn't feel right."

"Does it ever?"

"Good point." His expression changes. "Hang on, here we go."

I look over to see Ravens on the wing. Four of them. No, five.

As they fly closer, Wilf and I duck so we're better hidden by the tree. The Ravens begin to circle the bell tower protectively. Around and around and around.

Even from this distance they look scarily large. Which they are. These are not normal ravens. These Ravens are my size, made so by faerie magic. The Ravens convinced the faeries it would be better if they were made larger. That they could be more useful to humankind. And, for a while, they were more useful. But Ravens are clever. Ravens are tricksters. They started to wonder . . . what if?

What if London could be ours, to do exactly as we please?

The Ravens began to plot and plan. They convinced those power-seeking faeries to enchant the bells. And then, in one horrible, evil night called The Chiming, the Ravens got rid of their faerie allies, murdered as many faeries as they could, and took humankind under their control. The lucky ones (if you can call them that) escaped before the invisible wall went up, or dove deep underground.

"Here she is." Wilf spots Bes before I do and begins to unwrap the leather strap from his arm. "Gotta go. Thanks for the chinwag."

"Sure. And, um, good luck. I hope that . . ." I startle as Bes flutters above me.

"Stick your arm out," Wilf says.

I do as I'm told and Bes lands on me.

"Oh!" I say. I can't believe my luck. Does this mean she's warming to me? I try to catch her eye, but she avoids my gaze as Wilf ties the leather strap to her tiny leg. She keeps her attention focused on the bell tower and what the Ravens are up to.

"Right, that's it. Let's do this," Wilf says when he's done.

Bes turns her head and looks me straight in the eye. At the same time, she takes flight from my arm, digging into my skin with her claws. "Ow!" I pull back and then have to grab on tight to the rooftop to stop myself from slipping off the tiles.

"You're a bad bird," Wilf tells Bes as the leather strap snaps tight and he's dragged into the air.

I guess that's my answer right there. Bes isn't warming to me at all. I always thought I'd be able to tell her things. About school. Home. Life. I thought she'd get me.

I guess I was wrong.

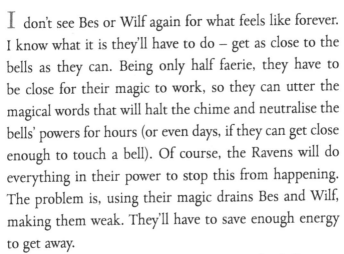

I don't see Bes or Wilf again for what feels like forever. I know what it is they'll have to do – get as close to the bells as they can. Being only half faerie, they have to be close for their magic to work, so they can utter the magical words that will halt the chime and neutralise the bells' powers for hours (or even days, if they can get close enough to touch a bell). Of course, the Ravens will do everything in their power to stop this from happening. The problem is, using their magic drains Bes and Wilf, making them weak. They'll have to save enough energy to get away.

There are even more Ravens circling the bell tower now. Just as I'm really starting to get worried, I spot a flash of brown down in the churchyard. It's Wilf. He's ducking from one tree to the next, gaining ground, edging closer to the church.

And there, in the sky, I see something small, darting and swooping low behind the church. Bes! The Ravens haven't spotted her yet. Digging my fingers into the tiles around me, I cling to the rooftop, silently urging her on. Surely she's close enough to halt the bells?

But she can't be, because the bells toll on, their solemn knell rising and falling as they sing their songs of hate and death.

I try to keep track of Bes, but she's so quick she's almost invisible. I only catch sight of her each time she makes one of her sharp turns.

And there she is again.

So close to the church now.

So close!

And Wilf, too! I see him duck behind a headstone in the churchyard.

Come on! My fingernails dig into the tiles.

The Ravens continue to circle, *cronking* and *kraahing* to each other, unaware that they have visitors.

That is, until both bells suddenly stop ringing.

When this happens, the Ravens instantly converge in a beating of frenzied wings, their *kraahs* becoming louder and louder, their beady black eyes seeking out the enemy they know is here. Somewhere.

I can't see either Wilf or Bes, but they must still be there. Hiding. Biding their time. Hoping they're close enough, repeating the precious magical phrases no human will ever know or understand. Gathering what little energy they have left to make their escape.

I tuck my legs into me to keep them from moving. From running. I want to go down there. I want to help. But all I can do is look on.

And hope.

My hope doesn't last long. I suck in my breath as I see one of the Ravens spot something at the base of a black iron lamppost. The bird cries a huge, throaty croak, and all the Ravens turn.

As one, they dive.

Bes takes off with a lurch, zig-zagging across the sky, twisting and turning as she tries to evade them. The group rises and falls, weaving in and out of trees, spiralling around the church. When one of the Ravens clips her, I gasp, but somehow she gets away. I lose sight of her then. And so, thankfully, do the Ravens. They break off, circling, crying out to each other, looking this way and that.

A shaky hand covers my chest.

They've lost her, I realise.

They've lost her.

I sit and wait, pressed into the shadows as the Ravens continue to spiral. I can't see Bes or Wilf anywhere. Where has Bes got to? Is Wilf still behind the headstone? And what about Kit?

I wait for what feels like forever. I begin to wonder if anyone is coming for me at all, and I start to panic. What will I do now? Where will I go? I can't find my way around this invaded London. I have no idea where Edie is, or how to get back to the real world.

"Let's go."

My legs dart out and I have to grip onto the tiles to keep from falling. I hadn't even seen Kit scale the rooftop, but there he is, still dripping wet from his adventures in the river.

"Come on, we have to hurry." He's already used a tree branch to swing down onto the little balcony below.

"Wait! What happened on the river? How did it go?"

He looks up at me. "Good. I only had to pull two Londoners from the water."

"What about Wilf? Bes? Have you seen them?"

"I saw Wilf. He showed me where you were."

"And Bes?"

"She'd already gone. They'll both make their way to the hideaway, in their own time. You know the rules."

I nod. It's a safety thing. They never return to the hideaway at the same time.

"Trust me. She'll be fine."

"I hope so."

"I know so. In the meantime, want to see something?"

"Um . . . I'm not sure."

Kit chuckles. "Come on, you'll love it."

I have to run hard to keep up with Kit. We make our way to the river and then slip silently from building to building, Kit keeping a close watch on the skies.

"Where are we–" But before I can finish my question, Kit grabs me and drags me around a corner and underneath a tattered awning. He points up and I look through the holes to see a group of Ravens fly overhead.

"They'll be everywhere, because the Tower's close by." He points to our right. "But we've got to hurry – the tide's coming in."

I nod. I know where he's taking me.

We wait until a group of marching Londoners has passed by a few streets away, then run again. I'm more artist than athlete, and my heart is pounding. I'm about to tell Kit I need to stop and rest when he turns a sharp right. He slows to a walk as we make our way down a skinny stone passageway beside a derelict pub and then down some worn stone steps to the river itself. The tide is out, enabling us to walk onto the pebbly, muddy foreshore.

"Look." Kit beckons me over to the edge of the stone wall, the brown water lapping at its edge.

We both peek around the edge to view the glorious Tower Bridge, black sentry Ravens perched upon its upper walkway.

Kit pulls back.

"You know where we're going," he says.

I nod.

"Then lead on."

I check for Ravens and then step out, darting around the side of the stone stairs and into an alcove that's tucked underneath. I pause for a moment to let my eyes adjust, and feel a drip of water land on my head. As I brush it away, a cloud moves and the sun shines down, bringing what lies before me to life.

"Oh," I breathe, taking in the ramshackle beauty of the scene.

The small space is encrusted with pieces of mirror and glass. Pinholes of light penetrate the worn stone above and the rays frolic and flit, reflecting off the glistening bits and pieces that Kit has carefully placed.

It's Kit's thinking spot.

I walk around, barely believing I'm here. In the silence, I inspect the old chair that squats off to one side, tied down so it won't float away. I touch a glittering teardrop-shaped prism that must once have been part of an impressive chandelier.

"It really is like a mermaid's grotto," I say. That's what Kit calls it. His grotto.

"Don't be silly. Mermaids aren't real."

I catch his eye and we both laugh.

"It's as wonderful as I knew it would be," I say. "Thanks."

He clears his throat. "Well, we had time. And I thought you should see it for yourself. See that there's still beauty to be found in this place. Despite everything. And I'm grateful to still be alive to see it."

I nod. But the truth is, I'm surprised Kit has brought me here. This is a private place for him. He doesn't even bring Wilf or Bes to the grotto. So why bring me, a total stranger? It must mean something. Maybe even that we could be the friends I always dreamed we'd be. Bes might not trust me, but Kit does. Wilf, too, I think. Again, I'm desperate to ask why Bes hates me so much, but I don't want to ruin my visit to the grotto. I guess I can only hope that I'll get a private moment with Bes as well. That we can get to know each other better and she'll change her mind about me. I go and sit down in the chair.

Kit's chair.

In the silence, I close my eyes and listen to the lapping of the Thames. A Raven's *kraah*. The distant chime of a bell.

My world. Their world. Our world.

I'm not sure how long I sit like that, listening, but some whispered words see my eyes flicker open again.

"Did you say something?" I ask Kit, who is standing over by the chandelier, watching me. I thought I'd heard him say "thank you", but in my dreamlike state, I'm not sure.

"Yes. It's time to go."

There's more running – a lot more running – before we stop again.

"Up here." Kit opens a door and starts up a set of stairs. "But I guess you know that, too."

I do know. We're heading for the hideaway. It's long been suspected (by both Ravens and readers) that the hideaway is somewhere in Whitechapel, which is where we are. Kit, Wilf and Bes have always been extremely careful about concealing its location. Before we entered this building via an open window, hidden from the street with a pull-down shutter, I noticed that Kit circled the block carefully. I realise now he was checking for Raven lookouts, trying to keep the hideaway safe.

After what feels like a million more steps, we reach the top floor.

"Home sweet home," Kit says, opening the door wide.

The hideaway.

I walk inside to stand right in the centre of the room. There, I breathe in deeply, absorbing the musty, dusty smell of the place. I take in the battered brown leather Chesterfield sofa with its missing buttons, the tatty green velvet chaise, piles of books, stubs of candles, and some old-looking bread that's probably been pilfered off

the back of a cart. And, of course, the large bloodstain –
Ash's bloodstain. I swallow, remembering Ash's greying
face. Bes's distraught one. I let my eyes skate over the
rusty patch, reminding myself not to stare. I can't even
imagine what Bes would do to me if she caught me looking.

I take a few steps forward, daring to reach out and
touch items I've only ever seen in drawings and movies.
I've imagined myself in here so many times. Closed my
eyes and pretended I was hanging out with my friends,
cosy and snug between bell raids. Pretended I belonged
somewhere. Really belonged. But nothing is as good as
this – the real thing. The only thing that could make this
better would be if Edie was here. I'd actually thought she
would be. That Kit, Wilf and Bes would be keeping her safe.

I sit down on the sofa and a second later someone
bursts into the room.

"*Cheep!* Comfortable?" Bes eyes me as she rises into
bodily form next to Kit. She clutches her left arm.

I jump up. "You're bleeding!" She must have been cut
by one of the Ravens – by a sharp beak or spur. I move
towards her, my hand outstretched.

"It's nothing. Don't touch me!" She ducks behind Kit.

A thump outside the door distracts us and we turn
to see Wilf enter.

"Great stuff, eh? Showed those Ravens. Not that I ever
doubted we would, of course." Then he spots Bes's arm.
He's across the floor instantly.

"What happened?"

"Well, there was this elephant on a rampage and . . . what do you think happened, genius? I got clipped, didn't I?"

Wilf is all business. He grabs an old biscuit tin and starts laying some items out on the small round table near Bes. He sloshes some sort of sharp-smelling liquid onto a piece of material and dabs it onto Bes's arm. Her jaw hardens, but she doesn't complain. The piece of cotton comes back crimson.

When Wilf reaches for the tin again, Bes shakes her head. "No bandage. What if I need to change form? My clothes might be magically accounted for, but a bandage isn't."

"But—"

"*No. Bandage.*"

Wilf sighs. "Fine." He throws the bandage back into the tin and misses.

The trio stand in sullen, uncomfortable silence. I pick up the bandage and put it back in the tin. It shouldn't be like this. Usually after stopping a destruction chime they'd be on a high. Celebrating. I think back to what Edie said when she first told me she was able to draw herself into their world. She'd said something about Kit, Wilf and Bes not letting her write the final scenes in the book. I hadn't believed her.

Now I believe her.

Making sure the sofa is between Bes and me, I find the courage to say something.

"I, um . . . I don't understand."

They stare back at me.

"I mean, a destruction chime is interesting and everything, but this is the end of the last book and nothing's happening! Where's Edie? I have to find her. I have to help her get home so she can get better and finish her book in time."

There's a loaded silence. Wilf turns to the others.

"Where's Edie? Honestly, this one's mad. She's stark raving mad!"

"I'm not mad. It's true! It's like the plot has stopped. The three of you should be getting ready for what's coming."

"The final battle," Bes says, her tone scathing.

I cross my arms. "Well, yes!" I say. "Everyone's waiting for it. You've got to storm the White Tower. Kick the Ravens out once and for all."

Without warning, Bes darts forward, scrambles over the sofa and grabs me by the shoulders. Her angry gaze bores into mine. "There's only one thing I'm sure of in this world."

"Bes!" Kit warns. "Be careful with her."

She doesn't listen, grabbing me tighter, even though it makes her wince with pain. "And that's that you're not welcome here. So get out, whatever you are."

Bes pushes me backwards.

As I fall, everything turns black.

My backside hits the ground with a thump. It takes me a moment to realise I'm back in Edie's townhouse – the one where I'd drawn myself into the London of the Bells.

I don't even try to convince myself that I fell asleep. I know everything I experienced was real. I get up and run to the wall. My fingers trawl the drawings.

They've changed.

My whole adventure in the London of the Bells is there. From drawing myself into the story to being seen, saved, and flown across the city to stop the destruction chime. There's my argument with Bes in the hideaway, and her kicking me out.

I keep staring at the wall, trying to take in what's just happened. What Edie told me about drawing herself into the London of the Bells turned out to be true. A part of me still knows that can't be right. That it's impossible.

And, yet, it happened.

I was really there.

I flew with Bes. Watched her dodge the Ravens in order to stop the destruction chime. Went to the hideaway.

Me.

I bring my hands to my face. *Me.*

But then my hands drop as I begin to remember other things. Like the fact that I still don't know where Edie is. And Kit, Wilf and Bes. They weren't what I'd expected. Especially Bes. All my dreams of our perfect first meeting – what they'd say, what I'd say – none of that happened. It was almost the opposite. They said so many strange things. Things I didn't understand.

They were obviously hiding things from me.

When they finally got a good look at me in the Underground station, they knew who I was. They even thought I'd be able to hear the bells from far away, like I was half faerie myself. But they also seemed to know I was from the real world. It simply didn't make sense.

What I really don't understand is why they hate me. Well, Bes, anyway. She truly, truly hates me.

I still can't believe it.

In my head, things are always so easy between us. It's like we've known each other forever. It's like I'm one of them. In Kit's grotto, I'd wished for a private moment with Bes. Like the ones I'd had with Wilf and Kit. I'd hoped I could win her over. Now I see I'm probably lucky that didn't happen. Without her friends to stop her, she would most likely have torn me to shreds.

I sigh and push back from the wall, dusting off my hands.

So, now what?

I glance out the window. The room is still as brightly lit as when I drew myself into the story, what feels like hours ago. It seems time doesn't pass in the London of the Bells in the same way. I hope that's the case. That would give me more time to find Edie and get her back to meet her deadline. She has to finish that book – write that final battle scene and hand it over to her publisher.

Oh!

I whirl back to the drawings. If I can see myself in them, I should be able to see Edie too, shouldn't I?

My fingers trace the drawings carefully, but there's no sign of her. Then movement catches my eye. I race back over to the drawing of Bes kicking me out of the hideaway. Beside it, the story is moving on.

The only thing is, I can't make out what's going on.

I squint and blink at the blurry, out-of-focus drawings, but they continue to shift under my gaze.

I realise the drawings are being hidden on purpose.

"That's not fair!" I call out, giving the wall a good thump. The blurred edges of the drawings ripple, like they're laughing at me. "Stop that!"

But nothing changes. Someone, or some*thing*, doesn't want to reveal the drawings underneath.

"You can't just hide things from me!" I yell. And as I do, I remember something else that's hidden.

The closed door that Edie didn't want me going near.

There was something about the way she'd spoken about it. Slowly, I walk over to it. It looks like all the other doors in the townhouse. But all the other doors are open. Every single one. This door can't possibly open into a proper room. It's down the end of the hallway, on the street side of the house. It has to be a storage cupboard of some kind. A broom-closet.

But it's not a broom-closet.

I know this door is important.

This door leads to something else.

Holding my breath, I reach out and grab the brass knob, twisting it.

It's locked.

I jiggle it harder, turning it this way and that. Definitely locked.

I try everything I can think of. I empty my pockets and try the key for the private garden. I stick a pencil in the lock.

Nothing works.

The townhouse is empty and silent around me. I consider the door for a moment or two longer, then shuffle back into the room I came from. I inspect the drawings, thinking.

What next? How do I find Edie when her world is conspiring against me?

I need more information. But how can I get it if things are being kept hidden? I could try to speak to

Kit, Wilf and Bes again – they were definitely concealing information. But something tells me Bes won't be happy to see me again so soon.

Who else can I ask? Who can I trust?

My eyes travel back through the story until I land on an event from the recent past. A gathering. A meeting of the Raven clans in the White Tower.

Hmmm . . . maybe it doesn't have to be someone I trust.

I grab the pen.

I draw myself into the banner room of the White Tower. It's different to the building that exists in the real world – this version has been modified to suit the Ravens and their human slaves. The banner room used to be the Royal Armoury – full of shiny, spotlit, historically significant silver armour and weapons. You could almost hear the clanking. The clashing swords. After The Chiming, the Ravens had their workers strip the room bare, providing a cavernous space for them to spread their wings. The banner room leads directly into St John's chapel, where the Ravens hold their most important meetings.

According to Edie's drawings, the chapel is where the Ravens are gathered now. I don't fancy being dumped into the middle of a room full of Ravens, so I decide to draw myself into the banner room, beside it – so I can get my bearings before finding the courage to go and confront them.

I land on a hard stone floor with a thud, the cold immediately enveloping me. It's freezing in here, the wind rushing through in great gusts. As part of their modifications, the Ravens removed the glass from the huge arched windows, for ease of flying in and out. No wonder it's so cold in here.

A raspy *kraah* reverberates off the thick stone and right up my spine. As my vision finally clears, I see a gigantic room before me. I almost cry out when I see six Ravens lined up along one wall.

But then I remind myself where I am.

I'm in the banner room. These Ravens are no threat to me, because they're stuffed. They're the fallen dead.

I rise silently.

The ceiling soars, built for Raven flight. The banners of the six clans hang from the ceiling – Corvin, Bran, Waldram, Fehin, Raaf. Brennus, the ruling clan, takes pride of place. The names honour the original six Ravens who resided at the Tower when the faerie and human worlds were first brought together. Now, the heroes of each of the clans stand forever silent and watchful under their clan banners. Each adopts a fearsome pose – wings outstretched, or head thrust forward, as if captured mid-battle.

It's horrible and thrilling all at once.

I hear footsteps and whirl around to see a set of stone spiral stairs in the corner of the room. I hide behind one of the Waldram Raven plinths.

The noise is made by four Londoners, each carrying a large platter of biscuits dipped in blood – the Ravens' favourite food. I'm not quick enough, and the first Londoner to exit the stone passage spots me as he enters. But it's all right. Like the Londoners on the street in Whitechapel, they don't see me as a threat unless they're told I'm one – they can't think for themselves. I hide anyway, cowering behind the Waldram Raven until they pass by.

Close up, the Waldram Raven is even more frightening than in the graphic novels or movies. Standing beside a human-sized Raven is very different to reading about one in a book, or seeing one on screen.

I eye him nervously, half-expecting him to move at any moment.

He's posed in what must be a most uncomfortable position to adopt for all eternity – wings pushed back, head twisted around, as if ready to attack whatever is coming up behind him. His eyes are truly unnerving. From where I'm standing, I can see his left eye clearly, and it stares at me with a fiendish sparkle. I'm sure that eye sees everything – even in death.

He looks so alive . . .

I can't help myself.

I reach out and touch the Raven's beak.

At the same time, a loud *kraah* comes from another room.

My hand jolts, and the top part of the beak breaks off into my palm.

I immediately panic. If the Ravens see what I've done, they'll skin me alive.

I frantically push the beak back into place.

Lucky for me, it stays.

I crouch behind the plinth once more and try to calm down. It's only as my heartbeat finally begins to slow that I realise just how stupid I've been. How could I have forgotten about the beak? The Waldram Raven's loose beak caused problems in book eight. Kit, Wilf and Bes had dared to enter the White Tower to save a faerie friend who had been captured. Wilf had bumped the Waldram Raven, and the top of the beak had clattered to the floor. They'd almost been captured themselves.

I really need to think harder, be more careful. I know this world almost as well as if I'd created it myself. I need to use the information available to me.

I wait, listening to the shrill cries of the Ravens as they fall on the food, bickering over it. At one point there's a particularly loud scuffle, then an ear-piercing screech that makes me cover my ears. That sounded human. After that, things quiet down.

I gag. I swear I can smell the blood, warm and metallic, wafting across the room. How can I go in there?

I have to go in there.

After a few more minutes, the Londoners re-enter the banner room. The platters in their hands, now covered in dripping blood, are empty.

But wait.

There are only three of them. Not four. And the third Londoner is carrying two trays.

Where's the fourth person?

All I can think about is that horrible cry I heard.

I can't go in there.

I can't, but I have to.

I look down at my grazed elbow. At the scratch on my arm.

This is not a good idea.

I run over to the next plinth, then the last one in line. I can see the entrance to the chapel now. It's large and open. Which means that as soon as I start across the floor, I'll be noticed. The thing is, I don't want to just stroll on in there. I want to make an impression.

I have an idea.

I run across to the last of the Londoners and snatch one of the empty trays from his hands. He doesn't resist, of course, just looks at me blankly and continues on his way.

I take a deep breath, stand tall, and walk silently across the floor, the icy wind pushing me on from behind.

The cries of the Ravens, talking to one another, gets louder and fiercer the closer I get.

Before I know it, I'm standing in the wide entrance to the chapel, visible to all.

I don't look up.

If I look up, I'll lose my nerve.

Instead, I take one last, deep breath.
And then I drop the tray.

THE tray falls onto the stone floor with a loud bang.

There is an immediate, deafening silence as every Raven in the chapel falls silent. I feel every shiny black eye in the room home in on me, burning my skin with focused examination.

That's the thing about Ravens. They are clever, curious creatures. They adore puzzles and riddles, magic and mystery. They will be desperate to know who I am and what I'm doing here.

I steel myself and look up.

The creamy yellow stone of the chapel is dotted with a row of arches that runs from left to right above the altar. In these arches perch the still, silent forms of inky Ravens, arranged in their clans, their colours displayed above their heads.

In the centre, above the altar itself, hangs the Brennus banner.

There is a swish of black. A swooping noise. I duck, my hands covering my head, and brace for the impact.

When it doesn't come, I dare to stand again and see that a lone Raven has settled himself upon the altar.

It's Coletun Brennus. The head of the Brennus clan. The head of the Ravens.

"Approach," he says.

I don't budge. There's no way I can trust Coletun Brennus. Out of all the Ravens who have held power, he is the cruellest. He'd happily kill every last Londoner and let the city go to absolute ruin. In fact, if it wasn't for the other clan leaders, he probably would have done just that already. Intimidated by his intense stare, my eyes shift sideways. And that's when I see the legs sticking out from behind the altar. The fourth Londoner. I'd guessed what had happened, but here is the evidence.

"*Approach!*"

I can't stall any more. I begin to walk slowly forward.

The silence above continues, as does the heat of the Ravens' unwavering gaze.

I'm still some way from the altar when I stop.

"Closer."

I force myself to take another step.

His eyes bore into mine, waiting.

Another step.

We are now so close he could dart forward and peck out my eyeballs.

One.

Two.

But not yet. Because first, he'll want to know why I'm here. Like I said, Ravens are curious creatures.

He continues to inspect me for some time. Up close, I'm surprised to see his feathers are not black at all, but a glossy, mesmerising mix of deep purples and blues – mulberry and wine, gunmetal and slate.

"What is your business here, girl? This is not the place for you."

I straighten my back, trying to look older. Braver.

"I've come to look for Edie St Clair."

There's a pause and then the chapel erupts with a cacophony of *kraah*ing that pierces my brain. I cover my ears again.

"*Silence!*" Coletun Brennus shrieks, half in English and half Raven's low croak.

A curtain of quiet immediately drops over the chapel. No Raven dares flick even a feather.

Coletun Brennus's hooked beak inches closer to me until it hovers just above the bridge of my nose. His head is cocked to one side as he examines me, taking me in from my feet to the top of my head.

I'm hypnotised by the reflection of myself in his mirror-like eyes.

"I know who you are," he finally whispers. "But do you?"

"I . . ." I stammer, thinking this is some kind of strange test. What does he mean? Has Edie told him about me?

Coletun Brennus stares at me for a long, long time. Then he pulls back, settling himself on the altar once more. Whoever he thinks I am, he doesn't seem to regard me as a threat. Which, of course, I'm not. I'm completely outnumbered here.

"I hear you've been on an adventure with our little faerie friends," he eventually says.

"Yes." There's no point in denying this.

"And did you ask *them* where Edie St Clair is?"

"Yes."

"Then why, pray tell, are you asking me?"

I'm no longer sure. Why am I asking him? Why am I here? Did I really think I'd be able to march up to Coletun Brennus and just demand he hand over Edie St Clair? I guess I didn't. Not really. I think I just wanted to be bigger and bolder than my usual self. I wanted to do something that Bes might do. Something . . . story-worthy.

I'm beginning to doubt my choices.

He takes a moment to reposition himself, his claws scraping on the stone altar. "Oh. I see. So the wondrous three didn't tell you they know exactly where she is? That she's been waiting for you to save her all along?" He pauses. Leans closer to me.

This is why animals freeze when they're in danger. I'm too scared to turn and run.

All of a sudden he darts forward, his beak to my face once more. "Perhaps it slipped their mind that they locked Edie St Clair away in a tower."

What?

"Or maybe your little friends lied to you."

Kit, Wilf and Bes have locked Edie away in a tower?

No.

I lift my chin. It's a dirty Raven lie. Of course it is. "I don't believe you."

His wings shrug as he resumes his position on the altar.

I want to repeat my words. I want them to be true. But I'm uncertain. I'd asked the "wondrous three", as Coletun Brennus had put it, where Edie was, but they'd never really answered my question, had they? They didn't even seem curious when I said I was looking for her. "I . . ."

"Yes?" Coletun Brennus is enjoying watching me squirm.

"They wouldn't lie about where Edie was. They wouldn't do something like that. It doesn't make sense. It *has* to be you. You've kidnapped Edie and *you're* lying about it. You don't want her to finish the last book in the series because you know you're going to lose to the faeries in the end."

Coletun Brennus tips his beak to the ceiling and cronks at this, as if what I've just said is hilarious. When he settles back down, he still has what looks decidedly like a smile on his face.

"But of course we will lose! In books such as these, the dark always loses in the end, does it not? I must admit

I find this most amusing. I'm informed that in the real world, evil often wins." He ruffles his breast. "My dear, we are, as your kind would say, resigned to our fate. But make no mistake, there is one thing we can still control – we can take as many of your 'beloved characters' with us as possible on our way out." He cronks again. "Oh, how those readers will cry and wail at all the deaths. Strange how we provide so much entertainment in this tale, but still no one cares for us."

I don't move a muscle as I catch sight of Coletun Brennus's firstborn son, Dolan, perching in the arch above his father. Our eyes meet, and he watches me very carefully, unmoving. If he knows where I've come from, he must be extremely worried about what I might do. What I might say.

The thing is, none of the Ravens – especially Coletun Brennus – know the truth about Dolan. The truth is that Dolan is a faerie sympathiser. He doesn't think what the Ravens have done is right. He doesn't believe they should have taken control of London in the way they did – driven the faerie folk from the city, massacred whoever remained behind, and enslaved humankind.

But there's more to it. Dolan has taken action behind the scenes. He has deliberately crossed his father many times.

He's a traitor.

I can't even imagine what the Ravens would do to Dolan if they found out. Readers, however – oh, readers love Dolan. It was Dolan who arranged for Bes's sister Marlie to be placed on that raft, surrounded by those beautiful white flowers. He knew what it was to lose a sibling. He lost all of his to his father's war.

The fact is that Coletun Brennus is wrong about no one caring for the Ravens. If Dolan were to die in the final battle, plenty of tears would be shed.

Dolan's black eyes look down into mine and he remains still. So still. I hope he knows I would never betray him. Never. He is the only good to have come out of what the Ravens have done. He is the only Raven who offers up hope in this dismal world.

Coletun Brennus stretches his wings. "Strange girl creature, this interminable waiting for the final battle is boring me. Go and see to the matter. We must get on with things."

I remain frozen to the spot. It's not possible what he's told me – that Edie's three most trusted characters have turned on their creator and are holding her hostage. And yet, somehow, I believe him. "If what you're saying is true, where can I find Edie? How can I get her home so she can get better and write again?"

Coletun sighs a raspy sigh. "Must we do all the work for you? Dolan!"

Dolan swoops down from his perch to join his father. "Yes, Father?"

"Convey our guest to Norfolk. Alive."

BACK in the banner room, I stare at the object the Londoner holds. He sets the strangely shaped device on the stone floor at Dolan's feet, places a woollen throw neatly beside it, then leaves.

"What is it?" I ask Dolan.

"It's an old saddle. I'm surprised it wasn't burned. Most of them were destroyed when the Ravens overthrew London. You'll have to help me put it on."

I lift up the heavy leather contraption.

Dolan points with the tip of a wing. "This piece goes over my head and this piece around my middle. And then everything is adjusted. You hold on here and your legs slip under here."

It takes us a while, but we finally manage to fit the saddle and tighten all the straps. I'm slow, my fingers fumbling with the leather, worried that this is a Raven trick of some sort.

"Tie the throw around your shoulders. It will be cold."

I do as I'm told.

"And now get on." Dolan bends down.

I hesitate.

"What is it?"

"I . . . I just don't understand. Any of this. Why I've been allowed in here. What I'm doing. What I'm *meant* to be doing."

"I'm sure it will become clear. In time."

There's something in his tone. "Wait. Do you know something I don't?"

He bows. "I know only what my creator wishes me to know. To do. I am entirely at her mercy."

I think about this. Maybe I am too. It's Edie's world, after all. But that's what doesn't make sense. How can she be trapped in her own world?

I throw one leg over and slide onto the saddle, placing my feet in the spots Dolan had pointed out. His body quivers underneath me. "Does it hurt?" I ask.

"It's not painful as such, it's more the degradation of being ridden by a human."

"Sorry."

"Ready?"

Dolan doesn't wait for my reply. We jolt forward and I'm thrown from side to side as he runs. Before I know what's happening, we hurtle through one of the tower arches. I scream and hold on for my life as we dive down into nothingness, then I cry out again as my head snaps back and we rise. Dolan's wings beat all around me and the ground begins to fall away. By the time we stop rising and set a straight, smooth path, I've almost caught my breath.

"We're not going to Norfolk," Dolan says.

"We're not?"

"Edie St Clair is being held in Suffolk. Ipswich, to be precise, in a bell tower outside the wall. A little calculated misinformation on my part."

"Aren't you worried your father will find out you're lying to him?"

"Of course. If he finds out, he'll have me killed. But I'm used to living in fear."

I'm sure he is. There is so much that Coletun Brennus doesn't know. For a start, he doesn't know that it was Dolan who helped the King and his family escape from London. Back at the very start of the Bells series, when the King was in peace talks with the restless Ravens, Dolan had accompanied his father on meetings. It was then that he'd met Princess Alice.

"It must be so difficult for you to see Alice these days."

"Always."

There's a finality to his answer that tells me it's not something he wants to discuss.

More comfortable in my seat now, I look down at the ruined city. Everything broken. Unloved. Grimy. Noticing me peering over, Dolan takes us down further. We're safe here, in Raven territory, on official Raven business.

"We'll pass through the wall soon," Dolan says.

I have to admit I'm a bit worried about this. "Do you think I'll be able to pass through it? I mean, I'm just . . . well, a reader, I suppose."

There's a pause before Dolan answers, and I begin to think he's not sure I'll be able to pass through either.

"I believe you can do anything you want in this world."

I wish I was as sure about this as Dolan seems.

"Here it comes."

I squint up ahead, trying to do the impossible – see the invisible wall. But something else catches my eye.

"Oh my goodness." When I look down it becomes obvious where the invisible wall starts and ends. Down below is a great divide. One side is uncared for and unloved – buildings and streets worn and torn, then a sort of no man's land, full of barbed wire and wooden barricades. And then . . . life. Something that looks very much like the world I live in. Normal buildings, cars, even a bus with people on it.

"Best hold on tight," Dolan says as he begins to climb higher. Much higher. "I must stay hidden outside the wall. My kind are not welcome there."

We level out just as we reach the divide. Even though I know I'm immune to the toll of the bells, I brace myself, half expecting to be slammed against the magical wall.

Nothing happens.

I'm through.

We leave the London of the Bells behind and continue to glide over the country I know – the one Dolan is secretly fighting for.

Both Dolan and Princess Alice want to return to the more peaceful London of the past, where the faerie and human worlds were completely separate, and Ravens were ravens. They know that life would be better for everyone that way. Well, for everyone except the two of them. It would mean Dolan being returned to simple raven form forever.

"Your father said he knows how the story will end. That he knows the faeries will win this war."

"Yes."

"But won't you miss everything you have now?" I ask him. "The power? Being so large? Being able to talk?"

"I'll miss Alice. If I'm even able to remember her," he snaps.

I tense, surprised. "Sorry," I say. Maybe I'm asking too many questions?

His body slackens beneath me. "It's all right. It's a fair question. I'll miss Alice, but everything else, no. Power, size, communication – it's nothing compared to the feeling of being free. I remember what it was to feel that way. Free of my father's rule. Free of human rule. Free to fly wherever I wanted. I believe this with all my being, as does Alice – everyone should feel free. We are both prepared to lose all we have for this."

He sounds so terribly sad. Tired and sad. It's not much of a life Edie has given him in this series, I realise. He's been so selfless and will be rewarded with so little.

If he lives at all.

We fly in silence for at least an hour, dipping and gliding effortlessly through the clear sky. It's nothing at all like flying with Bes, who had to constantly weave and dodge in order to stay safe. We pass high over farmland and villages, and cities with tall cathedrals.

"Not far now," Dolan finally says. "I'll have to dive in fast and find somewhere discreet to leave you. We don't want to be seen. Hold on tight."

I grip the saddle with both hands as we hurtle downwards through the sky, the woollen throw flying off behind me.

Dolan lands on a rooftop above a very narrow street. "That's the bell tower over there." Dolan points with his wing. "Kit and his friends are on the second level."

"And Edie. Where's Edie?"

"I must leave."

Just like before, I sense there's something he's holding back. Something he's not telling me. "Dolan! Please."

"It's best if you work it out for yourself."

"Work out what?"

"All I can tell you is that you're here for a reason."

"I know I am. To find Edie. To help her get home so she can get better and finish the last book in the series."

He turns a glassy eye to look at me intently. "And so what if she doesn't? Why do you care?"

"I care because . . . well, I love her books. I want to

read this one. And I'm the only person who knows she's in here, who can save her."

Dolan shakes his head. "There is more to it than that, but I can say no more. Only know that this is your story to tell. All yours. And tell it you must."

I have so many questions. But before I can ask even one of them, he's gone.

I sneak through a window into an attic filled with storage boxes and then down a narrow flight of stairs. I seem to be in a real estate agency. There are two people working inside. I wait until one of them ducks into the kitchenette and the other is busy on his computer. He looks up as I cross the floor.

"Can I help you?"

"Um, sorry, wrong office." I slip outside before he can ask any more questions, then take a look around. I'm in a row of old shops – black timber and white plaster rise up on either side of me. I'm out of sight of the church right now, but I just have to go up this street and turn right and it will be in full view.

"Excuse me," a woman says, wanting to enter the real estate agency.

I step to one side.

She's wearing a raspberry pink coat and her eyes are bright. I look down the narrow street and see similar flashes of colour and life – silver sneakers, people talking, a toddler patting a dog. Shop doors ding merrily as people enter and exit, going about their daily errands.

No one is enslaved. No one's eyes are dull.

A scraping noise across the street catches my attention. There's a man outside the newsagent's, closing up. He's bringing the day's newspaper boards in from outside. I slowly read the headlines.

Can the Raven Threat Be Contained? Prime Minister in Talks with US President.

Bridging the Faerie/Human Gap. Could Another Species Be Used Next?

Corvids: Should Earth Be Culled of the Threat? Expert Debate Continues.

I make my way up the street and stop when the church comes into view. The bell tower is pretty, the soft yellow stone punctuated with stern-looking decorative angels, their wings outstretched. Scaffolding climbs up the exterior – they're in the middle of repairs. I can see the bell right up the top and some shutters on the level directly below it that must be the belfry. There seem to be three other storeys below this, judging by the windows.

A wooden sign outside the building reads *St Lawrence's*. I wonder: why here? Why so far from London? Maybe it's some kind of meeting point. Maybe Kit, Wilf and Bes are meeting other faeries here for help, or advice? They don't receive much of either in London itself. Faerie numbers are seriously depleted in the capital and, of course, they are forced to live deep underground, where the bells' reverberations can't reach them. I'd be surprised if they were trying to raise a faerie army outside the wall, however. Without the Ravens' help in bridging the human and faerie worlds, faerie powers are weak.

Another ding of a shop door. The newsagent returns to bring in one last newspaper board.

Edie St Clair: When Authors Can't Finish Their Books

I read this headline several times. It doesn't make sense. No one in this world should be aware of Edie St Clair's existence. The London of the Bells should be all they know. I wonder if her being here has messed things up? It can't be helping. The sooner Edie gets back to her own world, the better.

The heavy, ornate wooden door to the church stands open. After one last look around, I cross the street and make a break for the church entrance. When I reach it, I dart inside.

I peer into the dim interior of the church, which doesn't seem to be a church any more, but a sort of community cafe. A man and two women are in there, cleaning tables and shuffling chairs around. I slide further into the building, making sure they don't notice me.

Immediately to my left is another wooden door, just like the one I exited in a rush at St Mary le Bow. Dolan had said Kit, Wilf and Bes were on the second level. My guess is they're keeping Edie on either the first or third floor.

Making sure the people in the cafe are still busy

working, I duck over to the small wooden door. The wedge-shaped stone steps rise steeply before me in a tight spiral. I start up them, being careful not to make a sound. Up, up, up I go, following the tight liquorice twist.

The first door I come to is made of heavy wood, with a round cast-iron handle. I press my ear to it and hear nothing. When I open it up, there are only stacked boxes and trestle tables inside.

I continue up the stairs. As I round the second bend, my eyes fix upon the next door. It looks exactly the same as the first one, with the same round handle. Behind it should be Kit, Wilf and Bes. This time, when I listen, I hear voices. One voice becomes louder – Bes. It's definitely her. I wait until I hear Kit and Wilf clearly. I can't hear Edie, though. So maybe I guessed correctly – she must be upstairs.

It doesn't take long before I'm at the third door. I go to reach for the handle, and then realise there isn't one. The door's wooden surface is absolutely smooth.

A door with no handle makes no sense. Hmmm . . . except when it does, because the handle has been removed care of faerie magic. I get down on my hands and knees.

"Edie?" I whisper through the crack. "Edie, are you there? Can you hear me?"

Silence.

Sitting on my haunches, I knock on the door quietly.

But my knock makes no noise.

Ugh. *Definitely* faerie magic.

I sit down on the stairs for a moment and think.

I can't get in. And Edie can't get out. The only other exit point will be the window. I think about the outside of the bell tower. And then I remember something.

The scaffolding.

I jump up and start my descent just as quietly as I'd gone before, but faster now that I have a plan.

I make my way down to the bottom of the stairs, slip through the cafe entrance, and run outside.

As I round the corner of the building, I look up at the scaffolding and the small middle window high above. It's not open, but I should be able to communicate with Edie through it.

The bottom of the scaffolding is covered with orange plastic. I sweep the end of it to one side and see a ladder. Within seconds, I'm climbing, one hand over the other. My clammy hands slip on the iron rungs.

I don't look down, worried that if I do, I won't be able to go on.

I've got to get to that window.

One more rung.

And another.

I keep going. Keep climbing.

Almost there.

I'm just about to reach out and touch the glass when

a small bird flutters above my head. "Go away!" I say, flicking at it with one hand.

It flutters again and I feel something fall on me. A sort of dust.

Oh.

Oh, no.

Immediately, I try to start backing down the ladder.

But it's too late.

Sharp little claws dig into my shirt.

I'm torn from the ladder and whisked into the sky, my arms and legs flailing. Then, with a swoop, we hurtle downwards so fast I think I'm going to hit the ground. My hands reach up to cover my face.

At the last second we dart around the corner of the church, whoosh through the door, and enter the spiral staircase again. There, I'm bumped and jostled and dragged upwards.

"Ow!" I say as my elbow scrapes the stone wall. "Ah!" My knees hit the steps.

Finally, I'm hurtled through the second-floor door and dumped unceremoniously on the wooden floor in front of Kit and Wilf. A gust of air, another ripple, a shake of wings, and Bes appears.

The door closes behind us with a sharp snap, and I'm alone with Edie's captors.

"WE saw you and Dolan," Bes says, staring down at me from above. "Could've picked you up earlier, but we thought it would be fun to watch you sneak around. And it was. Until you started climbing the scaffolding. What were you thinking? I could have been seen dragging you off there."

"Maybe you shouldn't have done it, then?"

"Eh, it bites!" Wilf guffaws.

I look from one to the other. "The Ravens told me you have Edie."

"You went to see the Ravens?" Kit says.

"Huh. Gutsy." Bes's eyebrows lift in surprise.

I'm secretly thrilled by this, but then I remember why I'm here. "I don't understand why you're holding her. Why would you do that?"

"Who says we're keeping her against her will?" Bes replies. "Is that what the Ravens told you? That we kidnapped her?"

I go to say yes, but then I realise Coletun Brennus didn't exactly say that. He said that Edie was in a tower, and that Kit, Wilf and Bes were with her. That's all.

Well, same thing.

"I'm disappointed you'd think that of us. Aren't we the perfect golden children who can do no wrong? The heroes of this fine tale?" Bes makes a grand sweep of her arms.

"That's why I can't believe you've done it."

"Even if we *had* kidnapped our precious author, which we haven't, we're faeries, not angels. We're not as perfect as you'd like us to be." Kit goes over to rest against the wooden table in the room. He crosses his trademark high leather boots, his trusty knife peeking out of the top of the right one. Wilf and Bes follow him, leaving me by the door, on my own.

Once again I feel like the unwelcome outsider. Well, I don't care any more. How can they honestly claim they haven't kidnapped Edie? She's locked in a tower one floor above them. How stupid do they think I am?

"That's it then, is it? That's the end of the Bells series. You're just going to lock your creator up, lie about doing it, and leave it at that. Leave everyone hanging. *That's* how you want to be remembered? A nothing ending in book nine of a ten-book series?"

They remain silent.

How can I get through to them? "Um, hello! You're supposed to be getting ready for the final battle! Everyone's waiting!"

Bes stares me down. Kit crosses his arms. Wilf sticks a finger in his ear and starts digging around.

I look at the three of them in disbelief. What is going *on*? They've fought so hard and for so long against Ravenkind, and now this, when they're so close to everything being over?

"I . . ." I honestly don't know what to say to them.

"What?" all three of them bark.

I take a deep breath. "I thought the Ravens had taken Edie. I thought they'd taken her because they were afraid they'd lose the final battle. But they've known they'll lose all along. They told me so. They get what's going to happen. It's only you three who don't seem to understand."

Kit pushes himself up off the table. "No. It's *you* who doesn't understand."

"But I do! And so do the Ravens. You'll win the final battle. Of course you will. I know it, the Ravens know it, everyone knows it."

"And what else do you know?" Bes says. "Who's going to die? Who's going to live?"

"Ha!" Wilf blurts out. "I know the answer to that one. It's you or me, Bes. You'll be all right, of course." He points a stumpy finger at Kit. "*Your* sort always is."

"My sort! And what sort is that?"

"You know, the tall, blond, good-looking one. The 'chosen one'." He does a little dance, making the floorboards creak. "Ooohhh, all hail the chosen one!"

"Don't shed too many tears for us when we're gone, hero boy," Bes says. "Don't make your pretty eyes red."

"Not a good look for the merchandising, eh."

Kit's expression is serious as he faces Bes and Wilf. "You know we're *all* going to lose in the end. The final book comes to a close and we're over. All of us."

The three of them begin to argue, but I can't follow what they're saying. I'm too caught up in what Kit's just said.

Is that what this is all about?

I point at Wilf. "That's why you were asking me what happens after the series ends. You're all scared of dying. Of ending." The words are out of my mouth before I can stop them.

In a flash, Bes storms up to me, her face in mine. "What would you know about any of that? Who have you lost?"

"Bes! Be careful what you say," Kit snaps. "We still don't know why she's here."

Bes ignores him, her gaze fixed on me. "You're a fool if you think we're scared of *The End*. None of us are. It's just that *The End* that's coming isn't fair. After everything we've done. All the raids we've been through. All the people we've saved. All the people we've *lost*. And all the while, the celebrated author is out there enjoying her perfect life. Don't think we don't know about her fans, the movies, her fancy house. And then to think she can give us a pathetic ending like the one she's planning? Caving in to what everyone wants? It's not good enough, so we're calling her on it."

Kit steps up behind her. "It's true. That's the real reason we're refusing to cooperate. We want a proper ending. The ending we deserve."

Wilf nods. "It's not the right ending. It never has been. And *she* knows it."

I'm taken back to the conversation I had with Edie in her study. She'd said something about not being sure of her ending. But still . . . to kidnap her. My eyes narrow as I look at the three of them. I get the feeling they're bullying Edie into writing the ending they want. And that isn't right. "But the final battle is all readers are talking about! Come on – there's always a big final battle in epic stories," I say. "Light versus dark. Good versus evil."

"That so?" Bes says with a grunt.

"You have to storm the Tower. You know you do."

"No, we don't," Wilf says.

My attention turns to Kit, who's begun circling me.

"And you?" he says, eyeing me closely. "What's your part in all of this? What's this got to do with *you*?"

I frown. I've already told them this. Why are they asking me again?

"Edie knew I could draw. She was worried that something like this might happen, and she knew I could draw myself into the story to help her if it did."

They give each other doubtful looks.

"What?"

They regroup, heads together, shutting me out yet again.

"Hate to say it, but I believe her. She really has no idea," Bes says.

Kit glances over at me. "What if she's actually here to help us? I mean, she's got to have appeared for a reason."

"What? You mean she's been sent?" Wilf replies. "By Edie herself?"

"Maybe," Kit says. "Maybe this is how we're meant to convince Edie to change the ending? Maybe we have to convince her by using this girl thing?"

"Hello! I'm right here! And my name is Tamsin."

They all turn to stare at me.

"Tamsin." Bes laughs.

"But it is!" Why is my name so funny?

Kit sighs. "Bes, we should probably be nicer to her. I mean, it's not her fault. She doesn't know."

"What?" I say. "What's not my fault? What don't I know? Who sent me? What are you *talking* about?"

I look at Wilf, who hasn't said anything for a while. Maybe he can tell me what's really going on here? But when I meet his gaze, he snaps to attention, stepping towards me and making me jump.

"You want Edie set free? You only have to do one thing."

"What? What do I have to do?"

"Run off back into the real world and come up with a better ending. The ending Edie *really* wants to write."

AND just like that, I'm dumped back in Edie's townhouse again.

"Ugh!" My eyes snap open as my backside hits the floor with a thud. Being kicked out of the London of the Bells is getting really annoying.

I jump up and go over to pummel the wall with my fists. "You can't keep throwing me out!" I yell. But then I fall quiet as I see something. The drawings that had been unclear before have now been revealed. There's the bell tower and the room I just left. There are Kit, Wilf and Bes staring out at me accusingly.

Run off back into the real world and come up with a better ending. The ending Edie really wants to write.

I step back and scan the surrounding drawings. Where's Edie? Where is she?

But she's nowhere to be seen.

Spotting the pen on the floor, I grab it and go to draw myself into the story again. But then I hesitate. What's the point of going back in, only for Kit, Wilf and Bes to throw me out once more? What's the point of returning when I can't get anywhere near Edie?

I re-cap the pen and sit down on the floor. I have to think this through. I know this much – all this fuss is about the ending. It's true that Edie wasn't sure about the ending of the final book in the series. She'd told me so herself. I take a deep breath, close my eyes, and return to that day in her study. What did she say to me? It takes me a while to remember. The first thing that comes back is how she admitted to being stuck, and that she thought she knew how the story was meant to end. That everyone thought it was going to end a certain way, but now she wasn't sure. Or something like that. Maybe Edie's characters are doing her a favour by calling her out and making her change the ending.

Or maybe it's not that? Maybe . . . maybe they're just scared, like I thought before. What was going to happen after book ten had obviously been on Wilf's mind back on the rooftop during our chat. Still, it's hard to believe they could be scared after all they've been through – their families and friends dying, the years of fighting. But maybe this time it's a different kind of fear. The sort that comes from not wanting to be separated. After all, if it's impossible for readers to imagine their journey together coming to an end, how must it be for them? So many readers will struggle with letting these characters go. It will be a hundred times worse for Kit, Wilf and Bes themselves. They've been everything to each other for so long.

I open my eyes and place the pen on the floor.

I can't go back in yet.

Instead, I get up and head for the door, quickly making my way downstairs.

At the door that leads back into Edie's other townhouse, I pause. The door is still slightly ajar, just like when I entered. I poke my head out, checking this way and that. Everything is quiet. I step into the hallway and hurry along to the front door.

"Ah, Tamsin! Thank goodness you came back. I was wondering where you'd got to yesterday," Mrs Marchant says.

I turn to see her bustling down the hallway towards me, but I don't answer. I'm too caught up on her last word.

Yesterday.

I remember she was wearing a lemon-coloured cardigan the last time I saw her. Today she's wearing a turquoise one.

Yesterday.

If a whole day has passed by, why isn't she frantic? Hasn't anyone been looking for me? My mother? The police? The first time I went to the London of the Bells, time seemed to pass slowly in the real world. But now a whole day has passed. That can't be right. There are rules about these things . . . aren't there? I almost laugh out loud at this. How could I think that? By now I should have realised there are no rules here. That would be *fair*.

This is a world that does what it pleases. That covers up drawings on walls. That spins time in patterns of its choosing.

"Did the lovely police officer let you in again? Does he have news?"

"I . . . don't think so." I answer her second question, avoiding the first one. "I just came to see how you were. And if you'd heard anything."

Mrs Marchant's face crumples. "I'm afraid not. Nothing at all."

I notice a stain on the front of her cardigan – tea? Coffee? She sees me looking and brushes at it. "Oh, I know. Look at me. I'm such a mess."

"It'll be okay," I say, trying to make her feel better. "Edie will come back soon. I'm . . . sure of it. But I'd better go. My mother is probably wondering where I am."

"Of course, dear. Pop back any time, won't you."

"Thank you, Mrs Marchant. I will." I run over to the front door.

The moment I'm outside, the journalists begin to call out. I ignore them and run, the police officer clearing a path for me. As I go, I tell myself the next time I cross the threshold of this house, it will be with a way to get Edie out once and for all. I've got to get her home so she can get better and finish her book. I want book ten to be real more than anything. As boring as I thought it was, I want my old life back. I want to be in my room, clutching book ten to my chest, safe within its crinkly bookstore paper bag. I can only see one way to make this happen:

I'm going to have to beat Kit, Wilf and Bes at their own game.

If we can't be best friends like I'd always dreamed, maybe we'll just have to be best enemies.

I'M nervous as I open the small door that leads into our basement apartment. What will my mother say? Where does she think I've been? Part of me is sort of looking forward to being told off. At least then she'll have to notice me.

But when I step inside, everything's quiet and still. Not a chair has moved. The kitchen is how I left it. There's no note on the table.

It's as if she hasn't even realised I've been gone.

But how can that be?

A whole day has passed by and my mother hasn't realised I'm missing? Unlikely. I know she's always busy with the house, running all over the city organising renovations, new linen, all sorts of things, but I can't remember her ever being away overnight.

Something is very wrong here.

Not only that, I have this feeling – even though everything is where it should be – that I've walked into the wrong apartment.

All I can keep thinking is that this isn't my home. It doesn't feel right. It's like when your brain tells you

you're at home in a dream, but you know it isn't your home. All the rooms are in the wrong places, and the belongings aren't yours.

I make my way slowly around the room, touching this and that. The pine table. A chair. I pick up a used eraser and inspect it.

They're all familiar things. And yet, they're not.

I shake the feeling away. I'm being ridiculous. Of course it's my home. Everything's in its place. Exactly where it should be. There's my room. My desk. My drawing things.

My drawing things.

I have work to do.

My mother's been held up somewhere, that's all. Sent on some silly mission to buy yet another crazily expensive item. Tiles made by ancient artisans in Morocco for the new kitchen, or something.

And while I know this isn't true, making up the story helps me push the thought of her aside and focus on what I have to do.

I go into my bedroom and take a seat at my desk. I begin to flick through the huge pile of drawings, trying to think of a new ending for book ten. This seems like the easiest way out of this situation. I give Kit, Wilf and Bes a new ending they're happy with, they give me Edie, and then Edie can leave their world and do whatever she wants with her book.

So, how could Kit, Wilf and Bes win against the Ravens in a way that doesn't involve a huge battle, or one of them dying?

Um . . .

Okay, so maybe my plan for a quick, new ending sounded easier than it is.

I don't budge all afternoon. I work and work and work.

And as darkness begins to fall outside, I've come up with exactly . . . nothing.

I've doodled for hours and now have pictures of all the important characters on my sketchpad before me. All the important settings. But I have no idea how it's all supposed to fit together. I might be able to draw Kit, Wilf and Bes and everything surrounding them, but really, that's just copying. I'm not an author. I don't know how to turn it into a proper story.

My brain hurts.

Exhausted, I give up and go to bed.

I don't sleep well. I toss and turn, my thoughts creating a tangled web of story. And then . . . it comes to me in the middle of the night, in a dream. I know where to go for ideas.

Nearby – one short bus ride away – is a tourist attraction called the Bells Experience. It's kind of like a cross between Madame Tussauds and a theme park. There aren't any rides, or anything like that, but there are life-size figures of the characters from the graphic novels, as well as sets, props and costumes from the movies. And I've just remembered something else there that could help me right now . . .

When it was announced that book ten would be the final book in the series, the Bells Experience installed a huge wall where people could write their own ending on little cards and pin them up. A wave of hope washes over me. Surely I'll find the perfect ending on that wall.

I$_T$'$_S$ morning and my mother still hasn't come home. I make up a story about a note she's written me that got lost behind the sofa. Or maybe it's fallen under the dining table. The thing is, she's actually had to fly to Morocco to pick up those tiles herself. They're needed tomorrow and no one else can be trusted to get them here on time. Yes, that's what's happened. Or something like it, anyway.

I'm sure by the time I get this whole Edie thing sorted my mother will be here and everything will be normal again.

Or not.

Most likely not.

But I don't want to think about that. There's no time to think about that.

I take some emergency money from the drawer in our kitchen, catch the bus, and arrive at the Bells Experience five minutes before it's due to open. I am seventh in line. The people in front of me (and those who soon join behind) laugh and elbow each other, excited to go inside.

At precisely 9 am, the sliding glass doors open.

The darkness quickly envelops me as I walk inside. People around me *ooh* and *aah* as they make their way down the short corridor towards the ticket booths. The theme song from the movies winds around us from hidden speakers, and everyone admires the walls, which are lined with fake black and white Tudor-style buildings. We are entering the London of the Bells.

I'm directed to a ticket booth. Beside each booth is a life-sized figure of one of the characters. As I pay for my ticket, I find myself face-to-beak once more with Coletun Brennus. All I can think about is how, just yesterday, the real Coletun Brennus had been so alive in front of me. How I'd seen the Londoner's feet sticking out from behind the altar, so very, very still. I shiver, remembering, and don't look at the figure again.

I push through the turnstile and walk quickly past all the exhibits, leaving the other visitors far behind me. I pass by the huge sets – the bell towers, underground faerie shelters, the mock-up of the raid on St Katherine's. I need to keep going – right to the end. That's where the wall is. I round a corner, still following the path. But then I pause as I spot something.

The hideaway set.

I come to a complete stop in front of it. It's all there. Everything I saw in the real hideaway. Everything I touched. Slowly, I enter the space and go over to the sofa, sitting down on it like I did for real yesterday.

The sofa is even more battered than it should be – so many tourists have posed for photos upon it. So many people have sat here, pretending they were hanging out with Kit, Wilf and Bes.

But me . . . I'd really done it.

Well, at least until I'd been kicked out.

As I look around, I realise the space is identical to the one I visited and yet nowhere near the same. Something is missing here. That cosy feeling of snugness that was in the real hideaway. A feeling of safety. Of camaraderie. Of family. Of *home*.

Eventually I hear someone's voice echoing from around the corner. I push myself up then. I've got to keep going. Got to get to the wall and see if I can find an answer that will convince Kit, Wilf and Bes to release Edie.

I round another two corners before I get to it.

The End, the words on the large wall read in a heavy Gothic font. A sign invites visitors to write their own ending. To imagine what happens to the characters in book ten. There are several raised wooden school desks that hold stacks of rough-edged cards and jars of pens that look like quills. Overhead, speakers play different voices that have been recorded reading ideas from the cards.

I walk past the desks and approach the wall itself, where so many of those cards have been pinned up. Each one holds a reader's thoughts about The End. Some of the cards have many words on them, others just a few.

I brace myself as I step forward to read them. Reading doesn't come easily to me. I know this might take some time. It's not something I'm sure I have.

I gravitate towards the cards without many words on them.

#saveBes is the first card I read. That fan theory again.

I marry Kit! another one says.

The next five cards I read talk about Kit, Wilf and Bes storming the Tower.

We all sit down to eat a fabulous dinner of roast Raven with all the trimmings, says the next one. It makes me laugh.

There are more cards about the storming of the Tower.

A smattering of *#saveBes*.

More cards again about storming the Tower. Readers really are incredibly excited about this battle to end all battles.

Finally, I get to a card that makes me think. *Princess Alice gets turned into a Raven somehow, and she and Dolan Brennus live happily ever after at the Tower.*

That would be lovely, but I don't think it's going to happen.

I spot another interesting card in a little kid's handwriting: *Kit, Wilf and Bes find a secret entry to the Tower and make a sneaky attack on the Ravens and win!*

And then another, from someone a little older. *Bes gets a faerie disease (like a cold for her, but the Ravens have never had it before) and she gives it to the Ravens, and they all die a horrible death with pox all over them and their scrawny little legs sticking up in the air. The End.*

I read as many of these longer cards as I can, because they seem to be the ones with the better ideas. When my brain gets tired, I sit down on a nearby bench and listen to the recording.

After a while, other visitors begin to file into the room, having caught up to me. Most of them read a card or two, but don't bother writing one. Finally, a family writes one and pins it up.

I'm hopeful, but it's another *#saveBes*.

A couple enters. They spend quite a bit of time reading the cards separately, finally meeting up in the middle of the wall. They look at each other, and there's something about their expressions that's thoughtful and considered. Like they're really taking this seriously. I shuffle to the edge of the bench so I can hear them better.

"What do you think?" the woman says.

The guy shrugs. "I know everyone wants this battle thing, but it's boring, right? I mean, lots of people thought there were too many raids in book nine. There was too much fighting and not enough fun stuff. I get it. Fights can be boring. You just start skipping pages, trying to find out who lives and who dies, you know?"

"So what do you think should happen then, if you don't want a final battle?"

The guy turns back to the wall and stares at it for

some time. He pushes his glasses up higher on his nose. "Maybe . . . maybe something from before. From the older books."

"Like?"

"I don't know, it's just . . . the books are so dark now. They used to be much more fun. Remember how there'd always be cool stuff you'd forgotten about? As in, just the tiniest mention of something, and then it would all be revealed in the next book?"

"Sure. Like the feather that Bes's sister Ash gave her just before she died? The one with the hidden magic?"

"Exactly. Remember how it was at least two more books before Bes's tears unlocked the magic within it? That was great. I miss all that kind of stuff."

"Me too."

"Yeah. Remember how cool it was when the faeries were always sneaking around, outwitting the Ravens?"

"I know, right? It's all so serious from book seven onwards."

"The story needs more of that sort of thing in it again. Some kind of sneaky manoeuvre would be so much better than a battle. Something clever that none of us has thought of, but that Edie St Clair has been keeping to herself all this time. It would bring everything back around to where the books started."

"That *would* be cool. Why don't you write it down and stick it up on the wall? You never know, Edie St

Clair might read it and realise you're right. They keep saying on the news that she's having trouble finishing the final book."

The guy laughs. "Edie St Clair is on her own. Unless she wants to pay me some of the millions she'll get for book ten and its movie."

With that, they stroll off towards the exit.

Interesting, I think, watching them go. I know what he means. I've felt that way sometimes, too. As the books progressed, they got so much darker as the war raged on and more lives were stolen.

It's starting to get more crowded now. I decide to stay a little longer, just to see what comes along next.

As it turns out, it's another *#saveBes*, an *I can't wait for the last big battle!!!!!* and a *Kit is so cute, I totally love him,* which is nothing to do with the end at all, really.

I've stood up and am getting ready to leave when it happens. A large group enters. One person quickly writes a card and then parades it around the group before pinning it to the wall.

"What's it say?" someone calls out.

A random guy steps forward to read it aloud. "Can't wait for book ten and that epic battle. Coletun Brennus is going to get what's coming to him! Storm the White Tower!" He laughs and turns back to the group. "Storm the White Tower!" he repeats, then points to the exit and leads the group off.

The group joins in with him as they follow. "Storm the White Tower!"

I watch them go, my eyes wide. Their enthusiasm is contagious. I almost want to join in their chant.

Storm the White Tower.

All these readers waiting for that final battle. Everyone wants to see the faeries finally take back the Tower of London. Storm the White Tower. Burn those Raven banners that have been hanging so long. Help the royal family return to London.

I told Edie that she didn't owe her readers anything, but now I'm seeing them in the flesh, just as desperate to read book ten as I am. Doesn't she owe them the ending they want? The one that will make them happy?

After everything I've seen here, I think Edie was wrong to second-guess her ending, and that Kit, Wilf and Bes are wrong, too. I wonder if the real problem is that Kit, Wilf and Bes are picking up on Edie's feelings? I mean, they're her characters. Maybe if she was sure about her ending, then they'd be sure about it, too?

Hmmm.

Now that I think about it, that actually makes a lot of sense.

I don't think I need to come up with a new ending at all. Instead, I need to talk to Edie, Kit, Wilf and Bes, and tell them what I've seen here today. How excited people are for the final battle.

I hurry towards the exit, which is through the gift shop. On my way through the gift shop, a porcelain figurine catches my eye. It's Bes in sand martin form, flying free, her little leather strap sailing out behind her in the breeze. I stop in my tracks and stare at it. She looks exactly like she did when I flew with her. Her beautifully detailed feathers are ruffled and she looks calm and free. Like she should always be flying. The gift shop is crowded, and people come to stand on either side of me, looking at the figurines. But I don't move. I keep staring at Bes, and I remember. I remember the air rushing past my face, my hair streaming behind me. I'd never felt more real.

"I flew with her," I want to turn and tell everyone. "Me. I flew with Bes, and it was *amazing*."

But I don't, of course.

Instead, I hug the secret to my chest and I buy the little figurine. Even if no one else ever knows, *I'll* never forget.

I'M lucky. There's a bus waiting that runs along Belgrave Place, which means I can get off right in the middle of Chester Square. It's not until I'm on the bus that I notice how oddly quiet it is outside. There's barely anyone around. Not on the bus, or outside on the street. It's weird. Not only that, but I feel so strange. Dizzy and sick and not right. I sit back in my seat and close my eyes, wanting the bus ride to be over. I really hope I'm not getting Edie's cold.

When I reach my stop, I jump off the bus and hurry along the street towards Edie's townhouse. I'm only part of the way along the row of sandwiched white houses when my step slows.

There's no one on the street here, either. No journalists at Edie's front door. No police officer.

Okay, something's definitely wrong. I've got that same feeling I had when I entered the apartment yesterday. That funny, dreamlike feeling. But I'm not dreaming. I'm awake. I know I'm awake.

Still, there's no denying it's eerily quiet.

Even more strangely, I see that the front door to

Edie's house is slightly ajar. I worry that Ink might have got out, but I can't see him anywhere. Mrs Marchant is also nowhere in sight.

I look around, uneasy. Where *is* everyone?

I cough, a deep cough that comes out of nowhere, surprising me, then I open Edie's front door. "Mrs Marchant?" I call out. "Ink?"

Nothing.

That's when I notice that the secret door is also ajar – the one that leads into Edie's *other* townhouse.

This is all far too easy. I thought I'd have to fight my way in here, pushing past journalists and making up excuses to get inside. Instead, I've been given a free ride.

I slink inside the second townhouse and start up the stairs, looking around me and listening as I go. Everything remains quiet. Silent. Still.

In the final room, I scoop up the pen and approach the wall. I uncap it as I inspect the drawings. Kit, Wilf and Bes are in the hideaway again. All three of them stare out at me blankly, as if they're waiting for something.

As if they're waiting for *me*.

I lift the pen to the wall and draw myself in beside them.

I must be getting better at this, because I don't land on my backside this time.

I land on my feet. Wobbly, but on my feet.

As the world brightens around me, I see that Kit, Wilf and Bes are still staring at me with the same expressions they had on the wall just moments before.

"Well?" Bes is the first to speak. "Have you come up with a better ending yet?"

Words begin to tumble from my mouth. I tell them all about the cards on the wall at the Bells Experience, how I'd sat there for ages eavesdropping on the readers. How I'd tried to come up with a different ending, but realised that the battle is what everyone wants. What they're excited about. What they're waiting for. The three of them listen with stony expressions.

"Don't you see?" I say. "You've got to let her go. You've *got* to let her write the battle scene."

Silence.

It feels like forever before Bes replies. "We can't let her go. We've already told you. We didn't kidnap her."

Kit uncrosses his arms and pushes himself off the table he'd been sitting on. He stands tall. "You haven't listened to anything we've said."

Wilf comes to stand beside him. "We're owed *our* ending. Our rightful ending. It's not all about the readers. It's about us. About us and . . . her." The three glance at each other.

I cough another huge cough that echoes through my body so violently that I have to go and lean on one of the hideaway's flaking plaster walls.

"I don't feel well," I say when I'm finally done. I guess Edie was wrong about her illness – it's definitely catching.

Bes eyes me coolly. "That's because you're sick. If you get any worse, the doctors say you might even die. Which would also be problematic for us, so don't do that. At least not until you've written the ending that was meant to be."

"What? What doctors? I'm not that sick. It's just a cold. Edie gave it to me. I *am* sick of one thing, though – I'm sick of you not making any sense."

Bes turns to the others. "We've got to tell her. Maybe we should have already told her."

I forget how terrible I'm feeling. "What? Tell me what?" I glance from one of them to the other, looking for clues.

Kit nods at his friends.

"Better get her to sit down," Wilf says.

"What's going on?" I say. "What do you have to tell me?"

The three of them ignore me.

"Try to be kind," Kit adds, grabbing Bes by the arm.

She shakes him off. "Be kind! Why should I? My sisters were murdered. I've been left behind to live without them. Forever. And I mean it when I say forever, because stories *are* forever. I'll never really die, even if I make it through to the ending. That's how cruel she is. So tell me why I should be kind?"

"Because she's like us. Don't you see that? She's more like us than she's like her."

Bes's eyes skate over me. As we stare at each other, something within her changes. Her expression softens and, suddenly, she seems less angry. There's something about this change that makes me feel even more frightened. What are they about to tell me? Has something happened to Edie? Have they hurt her in some way?

"Go on, then," Bes says. "Sit."

She gestures to the couch, and I go over to perch on its arm. Not because Bes told me to, but because I'm starting to shiver all over.

"Okay," Bes says. "Here's the thing. You have to know something. Something about yourself."

"About myself?" So this isn't about Edie after all.

"Eh, out with it, Bes," Wilf says. "You've never held back before."

Bes throws him a look. "All right, then. I'll just . . . say it."

But she doesn't. Not immediately.

I cough again. Everything aches. Right down to my bones.

"Bes," Wilf barks.

"Okay, okay! So the thing is . . . you're . . . you're not real."

I wait for more, but it seems like that's it. I laugh with relief. "Um, of course I know I'm not meant to be here. I'm from the real world. Like Edie."

"Well . . . you are and you aren't," Kit says. He takes a step forward and crouches to my level. "Tamsin, Bes *is* telling the truth. You're not real."

"You're a fictional character," Bes adds. "Like us."

"What?" I say. "That's . . . that's ridiculous."

"Is it?" Bes says.

I stand. "This is . . . just some kind of faerie trick. You're trying to trick me into doing something. Or saying something. Because you don't want me to help Edie get away from you."

Kit's expression remains serious as he rises. "I'm sorry, Tamsin, but it really is true."

Wilf nods, looking far too solemn for the hobgoblin that he is.

"What's worse," Bes continues, "it looks like Edie didn't even spend that long on you. Here, I can see you still don't believe us, so I'll prove that it's not a trick. Tell me about yourself. Tell me about the school you go to. How do you get there each morning? What are your friends' names? Your teacher's name? Tell me what you usually eat for breakfast. Explain why you always wear exactly the same clothes. And those shoes."

I open my mouth, ready to answer her questions.

Except . . . I can't.

I *can't.*

As each question hits me, I think, *Easy!* Except it's not. I have no answers for Bes. I know I go to school, but

I can't remember where, or how I get there. I have friends and a teacher, but don't know their names. I know I eat breakfast, but not what. And it's true – I do always wear the same clothes.

And Converse.

"What does your mother look like?" Bes's questions continue to batter me.

I open my mouth again.

Nothing. I have nothing.

What do you look like?

I'm not sure my legs can hold me up much longer, so I sit back down. My hands rise to touch my hair. My face. I remember the picture Edie drew for me of a girl with short dark hair and thick dark brows. And then I remember Edie St Clair's dark hair. Dark brows.

Her red boots.

My *red* Converse.

"You get it now, don't you? Part of you has known all along, really. You're her. A younger Edie St Clair."

Scenes begin to flash into my mind. Edie St Clair's reading problems. Our love of drawing.

How I somehow knew everything about Edie St Clair – what she ate, what she did, where she went – and how she always seemed to know what I was thinking.

The key to the garden that appeared magically in my pocket.

The fact that Ink liked me.

How I'd managed to draw myself into the fictional world Edie had created. How the London of the Bells felt more real than *my* London, which had begun to feel wrong – flimsy and weak.

And then all the strange things Kit, Wilf and Bes had said to me. "It's her, but not." How both they and the Ravens had thought it was hilarious when I said I'd come to look for Edie St Clair. How Coletun Brennus had suggested I didn't know who I was. How Dolan had snapped at me when I'd brought up Alice. How he'd told me this was my story to tell.

I stare up at the three of them.

"But . . . but I'm Tamsin," I say weakly, already knowing the truth.

I might be Tamsin, but I am also her. A version of her. A made-up, younger version.

I am Edie St Clair.

"Faeries love names, Tamsin," Kit says, crouching even further so he can look straight into my eyes with his beautiful green ones. "Names are loaded with meaning. Kit, Wilf and Bes aren't our real names. We'd never reveal our real names. They're whispered to us at birth – a secret between us, our mothers, and the universe."

I'm not sure I want to know, but I ask the question anyway. "And what does Tamsin mean?"

There's a long pause and then Kit sighs. "Tamsin means double, or twin. I know that's a hard thing to hear, but that's what you are. Edie has used you to get to this point, just like she's used us. And, like us, you're going to have to decide what to do about that."

I don't wait for Bes to push me out of the hideaway. This time I leave the London of the Bells myself. I close my eyes and wish myself back into the room in Edie St Clair's secret townhouse. And when I open my eyes and find myself standing in it, I'm not surprised.

I notice I don't feel sick any more. Because I know the truth now? I'm not sure. There's one thing I am sure of, however: I know exactly where I have to go.

I cross the room quickly, heading for the hallway.

The locked door at the end invites me to open it. Even before I twist the brass doorknob, I know it won't be locked any more.

I have unlocked it.

I have unlocked it with the truth.

Now she will have to let me in, and she will have to explain why.

Why?

I blink back the tears that are gathering behind my eyes.

The door opens easily, smoothly.

I walk inside.

"Tamsin." Edie St Clair is waiting for me, just like I knew she would be.

I look around. It is an impossible room. Where there should be a dank, dark broom closet, it is spacious, all-white and never-ending, with a long, gilt mirror on one wall that extends into the distance.

I know without having to ask that I am in Edie St Clair's imagination.

Edie St Clair is standing in front of the mirror facing herself, but in the reflection, she looks at me. She looks at me with the same eyes. Same hair.

She looks at me like her heart is breaking.

Like I care about her heart.

Why should I? She doesn't care about mine. If she did, she wouldn't have created me. I understand Bes's anger at me now. Why she'd hated me so much. Edie St Clair took her beautiful sisters just so the world would hurt along with her. So readers would hate the Ravens even more. Edie St Clair didn't care about Bes. She only cared about how she could make her readers feel. It's just like Kit said – she's used me. She's used us all.

I turn to stare at my own reflection. Here we are. Together. How can I not have seen it? It's so obvious to me now. That day, in the park when we'd first met. I'd even thought we looked a little bit alike. At the time, I'd wanted that to be true, but not any more.

I take a deep breath. I want this to come out right. I want answers.

"Everything that happened. I drew with you. I spoke to Mrs Marchant. A journalist. Police officers. I went to the Bells Experience. It felt so real. I felt . . ." I stop. I can't finish the sentence, my throat closes tight around the words.

Edie St Clair turns to face me, her hand on her chest. "You are real. You're as real as anything to me."

You're as real as anything to me.

I wince. They're the exact same words I'd said to Kit, Wilf and Bes when I'd first met them. Her words in my mouth.

"But I'm *not* real."

"Let me try to explain." She takes a deep breath that rattles in her chest, and then coughs, just like I've been coughing. "So much of what I've told you is true. In the real world, I'm struggling to finish my book. One day, I saw a girl drawing in the basement apartment next door. Mrs Marchant told me she was the housekeeper's daughter. She was completely oblivious to me – so caught up in what she was doing that the rest of the world didn't exist. I stood there for ages, and she never even looked up.

"She reminded me so much of myself at her age. My pen used to fly across the page and I'd lose all track of time. And I thought . . . well, I thought that if I could just return to that place inside myself, that I might know what to do with my ending now. How to finish this story. How to listen to myself and my characters, instead of being swayed by what my readers want."

I don't know what to say.

There is nothing to say.

"I really am very sick. I have pneumonia. And I think in this sick, feverish world of mine, all these worlds I've created have become mixed. I was obsessed with finishing the last *London of the Bells* book, as well as with finding that younger version of myself, and it all became horribly muddled. I never meant to hurt you. I created you and our drawing lessons because I needed to revisit that time when I drew because I loved it. Just as you do. But as soon as I created you, you had a life of your own. A name came to me, and then I invited you into the garden to get to know you, and you were so perfect, and . . . oh . . . I tried to tell you, to warn you – that day we were drawing in my study. But then you said you knew what the problem was and that you could help me and . . . I'm sorry . . . I'm so sorry . . . I should have told you then. Instead, I selfishly created the other townhouse – a way for you to draw yourself into the London of the Bells to fix my problems. *My* problems, not yours."

Of course it wasn't real. Who spends twenty-five million pounds on a townhouse only to draw on the walls? No one, that's who. It was nothing more than a feverish delusion. And I'd fallen for it, wanting to believe that Edie St Clair had chosen me. That I was special. I shake my head, trying to remember what I want to say – to loosen one thread of thought out of the hundreds that seem to be knotted together in my brain.

"Tamsin . . ."

That name. *Double,* Kit had said it meant. *Twin.*

"You made me trust you. You made me believe things about myself. That I'd get through school okay. That I had a mother. That I had a home."

"You will! You do!"

"I've never even *seen* my mother! All I have is a few notes." I wipe my nose on my sleeve. How could she? How could she do this to me?

"I can make her real." Edie St Clair stretches out a hand towards me. "Here, give me the pen. I'll draw her for you."

"No!" I push the pen behind my back. "No! There's no point. You can't just draw something and make it real. She'll never be real. *I'll never be real,*" I yell, the noise melting into the void.

"Don't say that. You are real. You exist. I created you because I needed to remember how it felt to not be pushed. Rushed. To draw for the sheer love of it, rather than for millions of people who don't always want the same things I want, and–"

"Stop telling me that! I don't care *why* you did it." I step back towards the door. "It's not the same as being real. It's *not*! I thought I was special and that you wanted to draw with me, and that Ink really liked me, and that I really flew with Bes, and–"

"Listen!" Edie St Clair cuts in, darting forward to grab me by the wrist. "Listen to me, Tamsin! It's nothing special to be real." She lets go and bends down to look me straight in the eye. "Think about it this way. The world is full of people. Everyday people with everyday lives, for the most part. They're all real, but in a hundred years, how many do you think will be remembered? Barely any. But if I say the names Peter Pan, Matilda, Pippi Longstocking, Alice, Oliver Twist, Eeyore or Paddington Bear, you know exactly who I mean, don't you? Some of them more than a hundred years old. None of them real, but each of them remembered. Cherished. Loved. So loved. That's real, Tamsin. That's more real than anything – to exist in people's hearts is to live forever."

Silence.

"You're a monster," is all I can say.

Edie St Clair laughs, a strange, high-pitched laugh. "You're right. I *am* a monster. I'm a monster who does terrible things. I hurt and kill people all the time. People who are then mourned by millions."

"But they're not . . ." I let the final word go unsaid, realising there's no point. I swivel on my heel. I can't stay in the same room as her. Not for one more second.

"Wait, Tamsin. Don't go. I need your help. Don't you

see? You're the one with the answers. You're the only person who can work out the ending this book is truly supposed to have."

I keep walking. "Then you'll never know what it is, will you? Because I'm never going to help you. Never!"

With that, I exit the room and slam the door behind me.

And as I stalk away, I hurl Edie St Clair's stupid pen away from me as hard as I can.

I go home. Well, not home. The place next door. Whatever you want to call it.

I bolt from Edie St Clair's townhouse and take the stone steps at breakneck speed.

Inside the apartment, I stand with my back to the door. I look around at the tiny kitchen and sitting room. Anyone would think it was real. There's the pine table with its four chairs, the stove, the small white fridge. There's even a whisk and a spatula lying on the dish drainer like they've just been used. Books, school books, drawing things, a TV remote. A woman's coat draped casually over the back of a chair.

Quickly, I cross the room and try to open the door that would lead upstairs, to the townhouse proper.

It's locked.

Of course it is. Not because I'm not allowed up there, but because it doesn't exist. Edie St Clair has only given me the basics. I don't eat. Shower. Get changed. See my mother. I live in a cardboard cut-out world, I'm nothing but a marionette with Edie St Clair tugging on my strings. That's why everything in the London of the Bells felt more real. Because it *was* more real. She's spent years creating their universe, while I live in a sketchy, quickly built, poorly formed set.

Why did I never question any of this?

Why?

I know the answer – because Edie St Clair made me that way.

I sit down at the kitchen table, but I can't settle. I feel like the walls are closing in on me.

I have to leave. This isn't "home". It isn't even close. I have no home. I have . . . nothing.

Nothing real, anyway.

So I leave.

I get up, slam the apartment door behind me, and walk.

The shadows tell me it's late afternoon. At this time of day, Belgravia should be bustling with life. There are supposed to be cars parking, buses rushing past, people walking briskly along the street, carrying groceries and exercising their dogs.

But not today.

Today, London is a ghost town. There are no cars, no buses. No people. It is completely silent. No bird chirps. No leaves rustle.

"Ha!" I laugh a fake, loud laugh that fills the street.

Edie St Clair has given up on me.

Now that I'm no longer useful, she's stopped creating my world.

That's how much she cares about me.

I wonder how long before my world crumbles, and I am no more.

I feel like a paper doll. Whisper thin, fragile and disposable. Loved for a day and then discarded.

I walk for a long time, mainly in Hyde Park, where I can pretend the quiet is more normal. When I get tired, I lie down and stare up at the sky. When I'm rested, I get up again and keep walking.

Is this my life now? Stuck here, by myself, in a desolate London? It could be, I suppose.

I am a nothing character in a nothing place. I have nothing to do and nowhere to go. I have no story. No goal. I don't have to find a magical locket, save a little brother, find out who has kidnapped my parents. Everything I have and know is either of Edie's world, or is built around the London of the Bells. It's all borrowed. I don't live in people's hearts. I can't live forever, like Edie said, because only Edie knows that I exist.

I exit the park and keep going. When I find myself walking past Harrods and see a familiar sign looming ahead, I'm surprised. I thought I wasn't going anywhere in particular, but maybe I am.

I'm going back to the Bells Experience.

I can hear the music blaring, whirling around the empty ticket booths and exiting the open glass doors into the street, drawing me in. It's the only noise I've heard for some time, and it sounds foreign and strange to my ears.

Slowly, I make my way past the fake Tudor buildings and the life-sized Coletun Brennus.

Inside, I ignore the Raven footprints on the floor that show visitors the correct pathway to explore the exhibition. Instead, I weave from set to set, touching what I want, doing exactly as I please.

I climb up high onto a platform-like device that the studio uses to make it look as if Bes is flying in the movies.

There I sit and survey my world.

It is all mine, after all.

I look down at all the different movie sets that have been dismantled and brought here for visitors to see. There's the hideaway with its tatty furniture; the huge banner room in the White Tower; a re-enactment of the raid on St Katherine's, where Bes's sister Marlie lost her life. Each one is like a miniature time capsule of a moment I know so well.

As I examine each of the exhibits in turn, my anger crumbles, and I begin to cry. I cry because as I look around me, I remember that I love this world so much. Each of these moments is more than it appears on the surface. They are built on feelings that came from deep inside me. Her. Us. And I cry, too, because I *have* to feel like this. Because I was made this way. Even if I wanted to, I couldn't stop. I reach into my pocket and pull out the little sketchpad that Edie St Clair gave me when we first met in the park. Opening it up, I bring out a folded piece of paper – her drawing of me, so like her.

"I hate you, Edie St Clair," I yell. "I hate you and your stupid bells."

But it's a lie.

I want to hate her. I want to hate this world. I want to walk away.

I want to be that paper doll that blows away on the breeze.

But I can't.

Now I'm here, in her world – my world – I see I can't walk away from this task I've been given. I might be angry with Edie St Clair, but this isn't about her – it's about the London of the Bells. This is *my* world as much as hers and I want a say in what happens to it. We're not one. We're two. And what I think – what I feel – matters.

I wipe my eyes.

I have to do this. Not for Edie St Clair, but for myself. I see now that I have a story after all and this is it. My tale might be short, but it's mine.

I have to give book ten its perfect ending. That's my story to tell.

But how to tell it?

I think about all the visitors I saw the last time I was here. About the couple and their idea for a sneaky ending to the final book. About the large group and their "storm the White Tower" chant. About this world that people love and believe in and feel so passionately about.

I sniff loudly as I stare at the hideaway set. It's funny, really, to think about the end. Because it's not as if those final scenes (whatever they are) will be drawn and the final book snapped closed. It's like what Bes was talking about when she said she'd never really die. The truth is, there is no ending to this world. The London of the Bells will go on. And on and on and on. The visitors I saw here? They won't stop caring about the London of the Bells once the final book has been published, the last movie made.

Of course they won't.

Those people – they'll read the books with their children. And those children will read the books to *their* children. And all of those children will draw and write and dream up their own stories set in the London of the Bells.

Kit, Wilf and Bes – they're not like me. Their story will live on.

I twist in my seat, looking about the huge hangar from my high perch. My eye follows the path through all the exhibits until it reaches the large red exit sign, which, funnily enough, has THE END written above it.

The End. That's where we all need to get to. But how am I going to get us there? I'm not sure yet.

All I know now is that I'm going to create this ending. Somehow, I have to get everyone to the final page. Kit,

Wilf, Bes, the Ravens, Edie St Clair and myself. All of us.

I have to come up with the perfect ending.

It's what I was created for.

IT'S eerie, walking back to the apartment. The quiet continues, the streets as lifeless as before. I realise time isn't passing at all now. It's still afternoon, and the shadows remain exactly as they were when I went out.

I push everything off the dining room table, straight onto the floor, and spread my drawing things out. Strangely, I can't find any large sketchpads – they've all disappeared. All I seem to have left is the one that I took out before – the small one Edie gave me in the park. There aren't many drawings in it, which means I have plenty of room.

Plenty of room to draw a different ending.

The perfect ending.

"No pressure," I say loudly, my voice echoing off the tiny room's walls.

I stare at the blank page for a long time.

A different ending. Not a battle. Or maybe a different kind of attack.

I don't know.

As the minutes tick by, the pressure in the room builds. The silence gets louder. The paper whiter. My pencil more still.

"Ugh!" I grip the edge of the table and push my chair back, standing. It was a mistake to come back here. I grab the small sketchpad and a couple of pencils and make my way outside.

I don't want to go far, in case I need some more drawing materials. So when I spot the gate that leads into the private park, I cross the street towards it. As I walk, my hand reaches down to pat my pocket. I know the key will be there, and it is. The little figurine of Bes is in there, too. I rub it for good luck.

Inside the park, surrounded by greenery, the quiet feels more normal again, just like Hyde Park had done before. This is why people escape here, after all. To get away from the busy streets of London.

I go over to sit on the bench where I sat next to Edie. Edie with her dark hair.

Like mine.

Her dark brows.

Like mine.

Her red shoes.

Like mine.

I tighten my grip on my pencil and sketch a quick line drawing of us from the back, our heads bent over our sketchpads, deep in concentration.

Our first meeting.

Her, me. Us. The same person, but not.

Don't get angry. Keep going.

I turn the page.

But what should I draw next? I stare at the blank white rectangle before me. I know one thing: I'm doing too much thinking and not enough drawing.

So I draw one bold line.

And another.

I decide I'm not following Edie's rules any more. Why should I? I'm not her. I'm me. My own person. I can do whatever I like.

I turn the two lines into Wilf, asking me if there might be a tree sprite for him after the end.

I draw Kit, standing in his thinking spot, shafts of light streaming in from gaps in the stone stairs above.

I draw Bes, confronting me in the hideaway, telling me to get out of their world. I can almost hear her shouting.

My mind freeing up, I truly begin to draw whatever I want. Quickly, and without stopping to question what I'm doing.

I draw a few lines that turn into a feather. Not just any feather, but the one that Bes's sister gave her before she died. The one with hidden magic that Bes's tears had unlocked.

I take my time drawing one large eye – Coletun Brennus's. It's so real it makes me shiver. *I know who you are. But do you?*

I draw myself, shocked, as the top part of the Waldram Raven's beak falls off in my hand, in the hall of banners.

Beside it, I draw the same thing happening to Wilf, in book eight.

I draw Dolan Brennus, sitting above me in the White Tower, watching me calmly. Coolly.

This is where I pause. I consider that picture for a long time. There's something about his expression . . .

Hmmm.

My backside is beginning to hurt, so I get up and move onto the grass, lying on my stomach.

I draw Dolan Brennus again, larger this time. That look on his face – he's trying to tell me something, I just know it. "This is your story to tell," he'd said to me. I draw Princess Alice beside him, and a question mark, before I decide to move on and draw something else. They've got to be important at the end of book ten. Their story needs an ending, even if it's not a happy one.

I draw some lines to see where I'm taken – or maybe the word is "guided". These ones are thick and vertical and I decide to make them into the tower at St Lawrence's, where Edie was (still is?) locked up. I suppose it doesn't matter if she is – it's not the real Edie who's locked up, but her imagination. I see now that Kit, Wilf and Bes were telling the truth about not kidnapping Edie. In a way, she'd kidnapped herself, to force herself to do the right thing by her characters. She'd known all along she couldn't give them an ending she wasn't happy with.

I draw some smaller pictures around the bell tower at St Lawrence's. Of the scaffolding on the building. Of the winding stairs. Of the normal street outside the church – a street in a town that hadn't been bullied by the bells.

It's as I draw the street, with its newsagent and people coming and going, that I realise I never found out the significance of that bell tower. That bell tower all the way outside of London.

I ask the same questions I'd asked myself before: why so far? Why St Lawrence's?

At first I'd thought it might have been because Kit, Wilf and Bes were meeting up with other faeries – maybe forming some kind of army. But that still doesn't make sense. They'd tried to do something like that before, in book three, and it had been a disaster. The Ravens had slaughtered them.

I doodle around the drawing of the tower. There must be a reason Edie was at St Lawrence's. It's got to be important. There's obviously something I'm missing.

So what is it?

I snap the sketchpad closed in front of me and get up. Then I run. To the gate. Across the street. Down the stone steps.

I don't stop running until I get to my room and find my laptop.

I throw myself down at my desk and type in St Lawrence's, Ipswich, Suffolk.

It takes me only seconds to find the answer.

St Lawrence's is special for one particular reason – it has the oldest ring of church bells in the whole world, dating from the mid-1400s.

That's got to mean something. It's got to.

But what?

I grab my sketchpad and draw some church bells with motion lines around them. Beside them, I draw a sign that says *St Lawrence's*. Five very old bells. They're definitely important. An important piece of this puzzle I've been given.

My pencil pauses on the page.

Puzzle.

Slowly, I put my pencil down. I start to flick back through my sketchpad, looking at all my drawings. As I take them in, I realise some of them stand out more than others. Some of them have a sort of . . . feeling to them. A magnetic pull. As if they belong together.

Like the ones of Kit, Wilf and Bes. The feather. The broken beak. And the bells.

It really *is* like a puzzle.

I rip those six pages out of the sketchpad and place them on the desk in front of me.

And I know it – I just know it. These are the pieces of the puzzle that make the new ending.

The problem is, I don't know what the picture is that I'm supposed to be making. I think Edie does, though.

I think, deep down, she's known the answer for a long time, and that I'm here to draw it out of her. To give her permission to write it.

I just have to piece it all together.

I need to find *all* the pieces and rearrange them.

Thoughts pop out at me from all over the place. I force myself to focus, to start from the moment I was created: when I sat at my desk, searching the pavement above for Edie St Clair's scarlet boots.

Just like with the drawings I have in front of me, bits and pieces of memory stand out. I pick up my pencil, grab my sketchpad again, and my hand starts flying across the page. I draw everything that feels highlighted and shimmery. Everything that glimmers and beckons for my attention. Even though the bits and pieces make no sense, I draw the disjointed items and feelings and things I've seen.

Being given this sketchpad.

Meeting Kit, Wilf and Bes for the first time.

The destruction chime ringing out from St Dunstan's.

Flying with Bes.

The White Tower.

The beak falling off.

Dolan Brennus.

St Lawrence's.

The five old bells.

The guy at the Bells Experience, who'd spoken about a fun ending. A sneaky ending. How he used to love *the tiniest mention of something that would all be revealed in the next book.*

I flip back to the drawing of the feather. What had his partner said? Something about hidden magic.

Hidden magic. Like the feather and . . . I flip the page back again.

The bells.

But that wouldn't work. It couldn't work. Unless . . .

I stand up so fast that my sketchpad falls to the floor and my pencil rolls off the desk.

Oh.

I know what it is.

I know what Edie is trying to tell me.

The tiniest mention. Hidden magic.

I lean over and grab book seven from my bookshelves. I open it at a point about a quarter of the way through.

I know *exactly* what I'm looking for.

I'm only two pages out. My eyes scan the page greedily, wanting to double check, even though I know I'm right.

I know I'm right and I know Edie is right.

And, oh.

Oh.

This is so much better. So much better than a final battle. It was never going to work. The faeries simply didn't have the numbers needed to storm the White Tower. The only believable way for them to win this war is to be cunning. To find a way to outsmart the Ravens once and for all.

And that's exactly what they're going to do.

I read the section several times over. And then my hand darts out, reaching for another book – book eight. This time I turn to a point about three-quarters of the way through. I read one other small section over, grinning as I go.

When I'm surer than sure, I snap both books closed and hold them high above my head, victorious. Yes! I hold the pose for just a second before I move into action, pushing my chair away from my desk and dropping to the floor. There, I grab my sketchpad and pencil from the carpet.

And then I start drawing, so fast I think I might just set the paper on fire.

I spend hours roughing out my idea. It takes quite a few goes to get it right and to fit everything in. Even then, I still don't feel it's perfect, but I know it's close. One thing's for sure – I have a new appreciation for what Edie St Clair does.

The moment my pages are as good as I think I can get them, I scoop up the sketchpad and run. I bolt up to street level, swing around the end of the iron fence and enter Edie's already open front door. I'm inside the other townhouse just as fast. I take the stairs two at a time.

When I round the last bend in the staircase, my eyes scan the floor for the pen.

There it is.

I grab it and uncap it, continuing along to the last room on the right – the one with the half-filled wall.

I don't stop until I'm in front of the wall itself, pen poised and ready to draw.

And then I freeze.

If I manage to carry this off, there will be consequences for me. With my task completed and no story of my own ~~ist in . . .

But I can't think about that. I have to do this. I *want* to do this.

I push aside the thought of my own ending, take a deep breath, and draw myself into the hideaway, where Kit, Wilf and Bes are still waiting.

I land in a pretty awesome pose, if I do say so myself – legs planted, hands on hips. Very Bes-like.

Or maybe it's not Bes-like at all?

Maybe it's Tamsin-like.

"I understand now," I say. "I understand everything."

Bes stares up at me from the ratty old couch. Kit and Wilf slump in their battered armchairs.

"I know that you didn't kidnap Edie. I know that in the real world she's sick, and that she's locked herself away. Well, her imagination, anyway. She wants that ending – the right ending – as much as you do. That's what she created me for. And I've worked it out. I've brought it with me."

"You've what?" Wilf says.

I hold out the sketchpad. "I've worked it out. The ending. It's all here."

Bes sits up. "You're joking."

"No. It took me ages, but I think I've got it."

They exchange disbelieving glances.

"Here. See for yourselves." I open up the book to

the right page, then place the sketchpad on the small wooden table in front of the couch. The table wobbles.

Bes makes the first move. She shuffles to the edge of the couch and leans towards the sketchpad. She doesn't pick it up, but she reads a page, then flips over to the next one, frowning with concentration. She shuffles further – closer to the edge of the couch. Reads another page. And another.

Without looking up, she beckons Kit and Wilf over with one hand.

Have I got it right? It feels right to me, but I know this is the real test.

Kit and Wilf come over to sit on either side of her. Bes takes them back to the start of my drawings, and after that, none of them look up again.

There are chuckles. Gasps. Pointing. Murmured discussions.

It feels like forever before they remember I'm even here. But when they finally look up, I know they approve. Kit's gaze meets mine, his eyes flashing greener than ever. Wilf flicks his beanie back and grins. And Bes . . . well, Bes looks like she doesn't entirely hate me any more, which is really something.

She might even look a bit impressed.

Kit stands, and takes me by the shoulders. "Tamsin, you really did it."

I try to keep my cool and fail. "I can't really take credit

for the idea. There was this guy in the Bells Experience, which is this sort of *London of the Bells* theme park . . ." I tell them the whole story.

As I get to the end, I realise that everything I went through was made up. "Oh. I guess there was no guy. Not really. It was just my imagination. Or Edie's, feeding me ideas. It was all fiction. My trip, I mean. Not the Bells Experience. I think that probably exists in the real world."

"There's no *just* when it comes to imagination," Kit says. "You could call us imaginary, but I feel quite real, thank you very much. And it seems as if lots of people don't care whether or not we're 'real'. I bet you're right about the Bells Experience. It probably does exist, and I bet it's popular, too."

Wilf puffs his chest out. "Course it is! My legions of fans adore me!"

"Yes, it's all about you." Bes rolls her eyes. "Throughout literary history, short, green, hairy hobgoblins have been the star attraction of every children's book series."

"You forgot tea-loving and biscuit-eating." Wilf winks at me.

"And loyal," I add.

Bes nods. "Well, he's loyal. I'll give him that much."

"Who cares if what you experienced was 'made up'?" Kit continues. "It's brought us all to the perfect ending. Us. Edie. You. The readers. That's all that matters, isn't it?"

I remember what Edie said about being real. About

Pippi Longstocking, Matilda and Peter Pan. What I'd thought about Kit, Wilf and Bes living on forever. And how I don't think I'm going to be able to. My throat eats my words and I can only nod in reply.

"You helped Edie work out what she really wants her ending to be. You helped her be true to herself, as an artist. And you gave her the strength to do it. Sure, there'll be some readers who don't like this ending, but that's okay. It's the right ending. For her. For us."

"Told you Tamsin could do it!" Wilf says.

"No you didn't." Kit and Bes whip around.

"True. But it sounds good, eh?"

Kit laughs, but Bes's expression turns serious. "There's only one problem," she says, turning back to stare at me.

Kit follows her gaze and his smile drops. "Oh. Oh, of course . . ."

"Eh? What's that?" Wilf asks. It takes him a moment or two to get there. "Ah," he finally says. "Right."

Kit nods. "Exactly. If we pull off this ending, what happens to Tamsin?"

There's no denying it. When this is over, I'll be of no more use to Edie. Without the search for an ending, I'm nothing. I don't belong in this world. No reader will ever know me or care about me. No one will draw me, write about me. Kit, Wilf and Bes will go on, their story told time and time again, but my story will be lost. I'll be lost. I exist only in Edie's head. As part of her. Not on paper.

For the first time ever, Bes looks at me as if she cares. As if we're friends.

Maybe it was all worth it, I think, *for this moment. To see Bes look at me like a true friend.*

There's a long silence before I speak. "The thing is, I've been thinking a lot about *before*. The time before the first thing I remember. *Before* didn't hurt. I . . . I don't think this will hurt, either. My ending, I mean. I'll just 'not be' again, I suppose." I try to put a brave smile on my face, but it feels like it doesn't quite fit.

"Tamsin." Bes takes a step towards me.

I smile even more brightly. "It's okay. Really. Existing for a short time was worth it. To see the final book have the ending it should have. To see you three get the ending you deserve. I know I'm not like you. I don't have a big story that spans ten books. An amazing past. I've thought all along I was a real person making real choices, but really I'm just here saying all of this – doing all of this – because I have to. Because that's the way I was made."

"No." Kit comes over. "No. I don't believe that. Maybe at the start, when we first met you, but not now. I think you're carrying out this plan not because you have to, but because you understand how important stories are to people. You know how real characters can be. And because of that, you care about our perfect ending as much as we do. Which makes you one of us." He places a hand on my shoulder and I feel its warmth. He's real. He is.

You're as real as anything to me.

"Yes, you're one of us," Bes says. "And we look after each other. Always. We won't leave you behind. We'll find a way to keep you alive, Tamsin. To tell your story. Somehow. I promise." She holds one forearm up at right angles in the trio's famous show of unity.

"We'll find a way." Wilf brings his forearm up.

"We always do," Kit says, joining his friends.

"Come on," Bes beckons me over with her free arm.

I shake my head. No. I couldn't. I'm not one of them. It's nice of them to include me. To say these things. But the truth is, I think we've all come to realise that after we act out this scene, book ten will end and I will too.

But Bes isn't going to take no for an answer. She grabs my arm, drags me over and slams my arm into hers, Kit's and Wilf's.

For the first time ever, I feel like I'm a part of something.

Like I *belong*.

"Um, thanks," I say, as we all step back. "I mean it." When no one says anything, I clear my throat. "Now, are we going to stand around chatting all day, or are we going to get on with this ending?"

I clutch the thin leather strap tightly with both hands as Bes flies us over Westminster Abbey. Over St James's Park. Over the London Eye, the famous Ferris wheel's capsules rusty and damaged. Over the crumbling ruins of Buckingham Palace, which the Ravens have destroyed. As we go, I try to take snapshots with my mind. I don't want to forget this experience. I don't want to forget what I was a part of, even if no one in the real world will ever know about me.

Before we set out on the mission, I tried to tell my new friends that I wouldn't be coming with them, but they refused to go without me. I knew it would be all right for me to tag along – that Edie could easily edit me out of the final scenes – but I wanted to give them the chance to spend their final moments as a proper trio. They wouldn't listen to any talk of leaving me behind, though. I'd tried to argue with them, but they'd cut me off every time I opened my mouth.

That's when I knew they really *did* think of me as one of them. It wasn't just words.

In the end, I'd agreed to go, so long as I could stay

in the background. Kit, Wilf and Bes would take centre stage, acting out the scenes I'd drawn and showing Edie how it would work so that she could draw it herself and finish off book ten.

The final book in the *London of the Bells* series.

As we fly, Bes keeps low, ducking and weaving. We don't see any Ravens at all.

"I don't like it," Kit calls out, into the wind. "It's too quiet. Something's going on."

"Of course it is," Wilf yells back. "This is The End. It won't just be us who are up to something. You can bet the Ravens will be, too."

Bes chirrups, agreeing with him.

I hadn't thought about it until now, but I guess Wilf's right.

My hair streaming out behind me, I look into the distance and see our destination – the Tower of London. And there, the White Tower.

Bes drops us off on top of an office block so she can scout around the White Tower and see what's going on. When she comes back, she doesn't change form, but hovers around Kit, waiting for the leather strap to be tied back on her leg.

"We're keeping on going," Kit says, tying on the strap.

Wilf turns to me, a serious expression on his face. "But before we do, I just wanted to tell you something, Tamsin. Something important."

"What's that?" I begin to panic. What else haven't they told me?

Wilf takes a deep breath. Pauses dramatically.

"You've got a bug in your teeth."

And then he cracks up.

After a moment or two, I burst out laughing. I give him a punch in the arm, just like Bes always does.

The strap snaps taut, we take off and Bes wastes no time in guiding us in through the huge arch that leads into the hall of banners. Miraculously, there has been no attack. No Raven has spotted us. There don't even seem to be any on watch. Something really *is* going on.

Once inside, we jump, releasing the leather strap from our hands. We run to hide behind one of the gigantic banners, and Bes joins us after she changes form. There are Raven calls coming from the chapel and each screech they emit makes me jump. I know they'd love nothing more than a faerie kill and, of course, Kit, Wilf and Bes are top on their most-wanted list.

I peek out from behind the banner. This is where it will all begin. It's not an epic battle that Kit, Wilf and Bes will be playing out as they draw towards the end, but an epic plan. If it goes well, the Ravens won't have much of a chance to fight back. It will all be over before it's even begun. Even better, they won't see it coming.

They'll hear it, though.

"Eh, look!" Wilf whispers.

I turn to see the three of them gaping at me. "What?"

"Your hair," Bes says.

I know it's probably a mess after flying, but since when have these three cared about hair?

"It's . . . different."

I drop the edge of the banner and run my hands through my hair. "Wait . . ." I pat my head all over. Where once I had the same dark bob as Edie, I now seem to have some sort of ponytail. "How? Why? What do you think it means?"

"You've changed. It's got to be a good thing, surely," Kit replies.

"Less like Edie," Wilf says.

"And more like . . . you," Bes adds. "It's a sign. It's like I told you before. I know you didn't believe us, but I meant it when I said we'd find a way to keep you alive. Maybe Edie listened to us?"

I touch the ponytail – my ponytail – one more time. I hadn't believed Bes when she promised they'd keep me alive. How could they? But . . . what if she's right? What if this isn't the end for me?

"I hope so," I say.

"Maybe you're meant to be a part of these final scenes somehow? Like a cameo role?" Kit says.

"Eh, I like it." Wilf nods. "I like it a lot!"

I'm not convinced. A cameo role doesn't make sense. I'm becoming *less* like Edie, not more like her. But there's no time to argue. "You've got to keep going. You remember what to do?"

The three of them nod.

I take a step to my right, moving aside so they can stand together. "Go!" I say. "Go! Make it happen!"

They move into action then, Kit and Bes leaving first and then Wilf, departing with a blown kiss that brings a smile to my face.

I remain behind the banner, watching on as the threesome slowly weave their way across the room, ducking behind the Raven plinths.

Finally, they reach the Waldram Raven.

Kit reaches up for its precariously balanced beak – the one I almost knocked off and that Wilf had dropped in book eight. His fingers are just about to touch it when there's a loud *kraah!* A flurry of movement follows and Kit, Wilf and Bes manage to duck behind their respective plinths in the nick of time.

Five Ravens exit the chapel, swooping through the room like shiny black bullets and exiting the White Tower.

The threesome wait . . . listening.

And then Kit tries again.

This time there's no hesitation – he moves like lightning. He jumps up, snatches the top part of the beak and is back down again in no time. Thankfully, the bottom part of the beak stays put. A Raven with no beak at all would be far more obvious. This way, hopefully the

Ravens won't notice anything is missing as they fly in and out of the room.

Kit, Wilf and Bes gesture to each other. It's time to go.

I run out from behind my banner and meet them by the last plinth.

The four of us listen for the flap of Raven wings, and wait for the right moment to make our escape.

We're not expecting a Raven to walk into the banner room, so we don't hear the claws scratching on the stone floor until it's too late.

Wilf sees him first, then Bes and Kit whip around. I'm last.

We stand in silence, the only sound the wind rushing past in an icy gust.

What do we do now? What does it mean?

Because the Raven standing there, staring at us . . .

It's Dolan Brennus.

DOLAN Brennus doesn't look shocked to see us.

He doesn't call out. Doesn't raise the alarm.

The four of us stay absolutely still as he lumbers towards us, his claws scratching on the hard stone floor. His deep black eyes don't leave us for a second. He pauses infinitesimally when he spies my hair and then what's in Kit's hand. He nods at me and his gaze moves up to the Waldram Raven's missing beak.

His expression changes then. He looks thoughtful, but not surprised.

When he looks at us again, his eyes are glazed, almost as if he's looking straight through us. "Send my love to Alice," he says. "Tell her that there will always be one faithful Raven at the Tower." He turns and walks out of the room, his wings drooping.

He knows. He knows they'll never be together again.

He knows this is the way things must be.

He knows I made all these choices for him. He knew about me all along and was still kind to me.

Bes steps forward, one hand outstretched. But Kit leaps forward on silent feet and drags her back.

"Dolan," Bes whispers as she's pulled away.

He turns and the pair look at each other for a moment. Equals in their desperate situations – prisoners of others' wrongdoings.

"I never said thank you," Bes says. "For Marlie."

Dolan nods.

And then he turns once more and is gone.

"I'm sorry," I whisper, as he moves from sight. "I'm so sorry, Dolan."

Kit drops Bes's arm. "Let's get out of here," she says.

Bes changes form, sprinkles dust from her wings, and the leather strap is tied on. We listen carefully for a few more seconds for any more Ravens, and then we're off.

I grab the end of the strap and we're out of the White Tower again. Bes flies almost directly upwards for what feels like forever before jerking sharply to the left. And it seems we've been lucky enough to go undetected again, because there's no Raven attack.

Not yet, anyway.

Time to move on to our next stop.

At least, I think it is until, as one, Kit, Wilf and Bes all jolt to a stop. Looks pass between them – something's going on.

Whatever it is, I didn't draw this into my final scene, either.

Bes circles back around and brings us down atop one of Tower Bridge's high walkways. Normally I think I'd be petrified of standing on an iron roof, high above the swirling Thames, but now I know Bes *will* save me if I fall.

"It's a bell, right?" I look between them as the wind whips my clothes around my body. The three of them had reacted in exactly the same way back in the Underground, when they'd heard that destruction chime.

Wilf nods. "We were just saying it's been too quiet lately. I mean, the bells have been ringing for work, for sleep, for eating – to keep the city running in its usual dilapidated shape – but nothing . . . unusual."

"Nothing for *us*," Bes explains.

Another look darts between them.

"More?" I ask.

"Three now."

"Four."

"Five."

There's something about their expressions. "Wait. They're *all* destruction chimes, aren't they?"

Kit nods. "They know we're up to something."

"Whatever this is, I didn't plan it," I say. "This is . . . extra. I'm only part of Edie, remember? Brought in to rediscover her love of drawing. The rest of her imagination is obviously still hard at work." Now I really question my choices. What if the ending I've chosen has set off a chain of events that will put Kit, Wilf and Bes in danger? What if it's not the right ending after all? I think about what Coletun Brennus told me in the chapel

– that, when it came to the end, he'd take as many of Edie's "beloved characters" with him as possible.

Despite what I've drawn, Bes may still not be safe.

I can only hope that Edie knows what she's doing and can successfully combine both our ideas into the perfect ending for her series.

"Six."

"Seven."

"Eight."

"What? They're all ringing at once?" I ask. My teeth begin to chatter. Kit notices and hugs me to his side for warmth.

"The Ravens are obviously trying to flush us out for some reason. All of us." Kit looks out over the river. "The faeries in hiding will find out that all these destruction chimes are ringing. They always have at least one person on watch in each sector. They won't be able to stay away."

"The Ravens have a plan all right," Wilf groans. "And it's not going to be a nice one."

"When has it ever been a nice one?" Bes snorts.

"Eh, you never know. They could be planning a surprise party for us, and this is our invitation. There might be jelly and Pin the Tail on the Donkey."

"More like Pin Our Heads to the White Tower."

As they bicker, I try to get a grip on my thoughts. I'd been so sure of this plan moments ago. Am I still? I don't know. I think so. I guess the best I can do is to look like I'm sure. I have to help Kit, Wilf and Bes follow this through to the end.

I take a deep breath. "Look, if you believe in this ending, you've got to be quick. What if one of the Ravens spots the missing beak and starts to wonder? And don't forget the Londoners. And the faeries. Now all those destruction chimes are ringing, there's no time for standing around and talking."

"Tamsin's right," Bes says. "We've got to move. *Now.*" Her final word comes out in a chirp, because she's already changed form and is sprinkling us with dust.

WE fly on for what feels like forever.

It begins to rain, but we keep going. We have to. People are counting on us. As my teeth continue to chatter and my body is overcome with shivers, I try to warm myself with the thought that when I asked Kit, Wilf and Bes if they believed in this ending, not one of them questioned it for a second.

We're passing over a small village, the square gothic tower of the local church in sight. I'm so cold that my bones ache.

Out of nowhere, something black enters my field of vision. I turn my head, but by the time I realise what's happening, I'm hit with a force that pushes me roughly to one side. A dark wing snaps in my face and I scream, almost dropping the leather strap. I look up to see a Raven circling back around. We're under attack.

"Hold on!" Wilf yells at me from above, a stripe of blood on his cheek that wasn't there before.

I make sure my hand is wrapped tightly in the strap, frantically looking around to see if it's a lone Raven or if there are more. I can't see any others – there are no more black slashes in the sky. Just this one, huge and menacing, fast approaching again.

I cry out as I unexpectedly begin to freefall, Bes dropping fast. And just in time, because the Raven swoops from above. There's a huge tug that pulls my head back, wrenching my shoulder and then we're off again, up, up, up, the cold rain driving into my eyes and blinding me. I can't see anything – where we're going, where the Raven is, or if more are coming. All I can do is hope that Bes knows what she's doing.

Bes knows what she's doing, I tell myself.

A stone wall appears suddenly through the thick rain and then, with a *whump* and a thud, I land hard on something and skid painfully to a stop, the leather strap whipping back and lashing me in the face.

Someone grabs me and pushes me into a corner. It's only then that I work out we're on top of the square church tower I'd seen before. Kit hurls himself into the corner beside me, then Wilf, so we're squashed in like sardines.

"Keep low," Kit says. "We can't be seen."

"Where's Bes?" I begin to panic, trying to get up to look for her. "Where is she?"

"She'll be all right." Wilf grips my arm tight, making sure I stay down. "Legs in, eh," he says, and I pull them into my chest.

"It's just the one Raven," Kit tells me. "He must have followed us from London. Bes will get rid of him."

I close my eyes and sink my head into my knees. But what if she can't? What if I was wrong? What if I can't save Bes?

Kit taps me on the arm.

"It'll be okay. It's just . . . there has to be excitement. This is the end, remember? It'll be great. Bes will be out there, doing some crazy flying. Getting attacked. Almost dying. I bet we'll *all* come close to dying in these last few scenes. It's the way it has to be. Maybe you'll be next?" He grins at Wilf.

"You've always been such a great friend," Wilf says.

I look up at the sky, but can't see any sign of Bes. Let's hope it's just "almost dying" we're dealing with here. Not the real thing.

Maybe Kit and Wilf are more worried than they seem, because we sit in silence after that, the rain beating down relentlessly. Eventually it stops and the sky clears.

And still no Bes.

No Bes and, all the while, faeries and Londoners are being marched to their deaths.

My face turned upwards, I begin to chant in my head. *Come on, Bes.*

It can't end this way for her. She's come so far. Been through so much.

Come on, Bes. Come on.

"Look! There she is!" Kit cries out as I see a flash of movement in the sky above.

Something follows.

Something large and black.

"Oh . . ." I breathe as my eyes follow the pair across the sky. Up and down they go, dipping and weaving in a horrible, deadly dance.

Come on, Bes. Come on.

Up they go again, so impossibly high I'm about to cry out. The darkness seems to be closing in on her. Up, up, up.

And then down.

Down too fast.

I gasp. "No! He's got her. He's got her!"

Down, down, down.

Until both birds disappear from view.

I go to stand, but Wilf pulls me down. "Sit!"

"She can do this," Kit says. "Trust her."

I glare at him. He doesn't understand. I've *always* trusted Bes. I've always known she had it in her to make it through the series and I desperately wanted her to. What I didn't know was if the Ravens would let her. And now . . . oh, I can't bear it. The Raven's clipped her. She's falling.

Fallen.

Gone.

Just like her sisters before her.

But that's when I hear it – the beating of small wings – and I feel the sharp little claws come to rest on my shoulder.

Bes!

She chirrups and flies off, changing form to rise above us.

"I finally managed to outmanoeuvre him," she says, as soon as she can speak. Kit and Wilf jump up and bring her over to sit down next to me. "But it got ugly." She gestures towards her foot, which is turned painfully inwards. It's obviously broken.

"Oh, Bes! No!" I say.

She shrugs. "Hey, you should see the other guy. Let's just say he had a date with a tree."

I can't stop looking at her foot, and Bes catches my horrified expression. "It's okay. It'll be okay," she says, though her grimace says otherwise. "At least it wasn't a wing. I'll be needing those."

Wilf sighs. "And at least there was only one Raven."

"Er, about that. Bad news," Bes says.

"*What?*" we all say at once.

"There was another Raven, as it turns out. Circling higher up. He took off when he realised his friend wasn't going to win. Which means we've got to get on with this before he comes back with his friends."

Kit is already on his feet.

"But . . ." I say. I know she's right. I feel guilty, because I know I caused her this pain. Or a version of myself did. "I'm sorry," I tell her, knowing things are only going to get worse.

"It's all right," Bes says. "Hey, a broken foot's better

than dying. I guess I've got you to thank for that." She chirrups as she changes form again.

But it's not all right, and I feel terrible as Kit attaches the leather strap to her good leg.

I called Edie a monster.

That monster is me.

I did this to her.

But also, together, I think we somehow just managed to save Bes.

We fly the rest of the way without incident, though we go a lot slower. I can tell Bes is in pain, and carrying the three of us isn't helping any.

When we get to our destination, Bes circles around. She makes a first attempt to set us down close to where we need to be, but at the last moment, a woman walking in the street catches sight of us and calls out. There's immediate panic – screams and people running everywhere. Being outside of the magical wall, these people are always on alert. Always worried that they, too, will soon be under the spell of the bells and the Ravens. Bes has no other option but to take off again. She flies several streets away and finds a quieter spot to land, in the old graveyard of another nearby church.

"Cheery," Wilf says, looking around as we wait for Bes to change form.

When she does, she immediately falls to the ground,

her usually brown, healthy face far paler than it should be. The three of us lunge forward to pick her up, but Bes holds up a hand.

"I'll hide here," she says. "I don't have the energy to change form again, and I can't walk. You've got to go on without me."

"Not likely," Wilf says.

"We'll carry you," Kit says. "St Lawrence's isn't far."

That's where we're going. We need to get to St Lawrence's and its ring of five special bells. The only problem is, we've been spotted now. Everyone will be looking for us and my new friends don't exactly blend in. Kit's shock of white hair and high leather boots are an interesting combination for downtown Ipswich. Bes looks . . . well . . . feathery, at the best of times. And then there's Wilf. Squat, hairy, greenish and knobbly like the half hobgoblin he is.

Somehow, we need to get to St Lawrence's without being seen, captured and stoned to death. Or worse. Though I'm not sure what worse is.

I don't know what to do. I don't have all the answers. I don't know why that woman saw us, meaning we ended up here, in the wrong churchyard. I don't know why the Ravens attacked us on our way, or why Dolan Brennus walked in on us in the White Tower, or how Kit, Wilf and Bes will even recall the loose Waldram Raven beak and get this plan happening. I didn't draw any of this.

Edie did. Or will. All I can do is try to pull off this one little bit of the story, and see what happens.

A drop of rain falls onto my forehead.

"Eh, wouldn't you know it," Wilf says, looking up as the rain begins to fall again.

But it gives me an idea.

"Wait here," I say.

I run around to the front of the church. Please, I think. Please let me be right.

And I am.

There, in a tall stand by the church's large wooden door, are a number of left-behind umbrellas. I grab two large golf umbrellas – one with the Union Jack all over it, and one patterned with tiny flamingos, of all things – and race back to the group, opening up the umbrellas as I go.

"Subtle," Wilf says.

"But a very good idea," Kit adds.

I feel a tap on my foot and look down to see Bes grinning up at me through a pain-filled grimace.

"How about that? The umbrella matches your shoes."

I stare at them. My shoes. They're not red any more. Now I'm wearing hot pink Converse. I have a ponytail and hot pink Converse. I look at Bes. At Wilf. At Kit.

"You're going to be okay," Kit says.

I hadn't believed it before. I'd thought maybe the ponytail was a mistake. A glitch. But now . . . all these changes. They've *got* to mean something. Finally, I let myself begin to believe it. That maybe Kit's right and I'm going to survive this. The thing is, though, if I'm not a younger version of Edie any more, then who am I? What am I?

And the big question, of course, is: where do I belong?

USING the umbrellas as shields, we make our way down the street towards St Lawrence's as quickly as we can, Bes hobbling between us. The panic has worked in our favour – almost everyone has deserted the area. Still, it will only take one person to notice us and we'll be set upon. Kit, Wilf and Bes aren't welcome here, even if they *have* come to save everyone.

The buildings close in overhead as the street narrows and the tower of St Lawrence's comes into sight. It's impossible to walk four abreast now, so we have to split into pairs. This isn't good. It's harder to angle the umbrellas and keep hidden, and there are more people here. The brave and curious who have stayed after the faerie sighting have gathered together and are standing around in small groups, talking and looking up at the sky.

We make it all the way up to the church door before we're spotted.

"Look! With the umbrellas! That's them!" a man shouts.

Kit swears under his breath as we fall inside the open front door of the church. He slams it behind us, bolting it closed. "We've got to hurry," he says. "There'll be a mob coming our way shortly." He hustles us towards the stairs that rise to the bell tower.

At the last moment, I spot the cafe chairs and run across the floor to grab one. I drag it back with me and wrestle it into the stairwell. It's awkward, but I manage to close the door and wedge the chair behind it.

"It should hold for a while," I tell the others, wondering how Edie will re-write all of this. This is their story, not mine. Wilf will have wedged that chair into place, not me. Kit will have had the idea about the umbrellas. I don't know what Edie's doing to me – why I'm changing – but I know that ponytails and hot pink Converse don't belong in the medieval-looking London of the Bells. What's important now is that they hurry. They have to complete their mission before the mob attacks and stops them. Before the missing Raven alerts its clan and doubles back. Before all the faeries and the Londoners are drowned in the Thames.

"Run, Kit," Wilf says. "Straight to the belfry. I'll help Bes up to the ringing chamber."

"But the bell will ring itself once I inscribe the words."

"But we can help it ring faster and louder, eh?"

"Good idea."

"Eh, they don't call me the smart, handsome one for nothing."

Despite her pain, Bes snorts.

Kit whips the Waldram Raven's beak out of his tunic.

"I'm already gone," he replies. And he is, his long legs taking him around the next twist of the stairs in no time.

Wilf and I slowly help Bes up the stairs to the ringing chamber. There, in a small stone room, five thick white swirls of rope hang through the wooden ceiling. A flourish of red, white and blue cord indicates the part to be pulled.

"Here we go," Wilf says, helping her sit down, her back against one of the stone walls. She looks very pasty again, so much so that I wonder if she has other injuries she hasn't told us about. I think Wilf senses this, too, because his large frame hovers above her nervously. "Kit won't be long. He'll get the job done."

Bes nods, leans her head back against the wall and closes her eyes.

"That's it. Rest now."

Bes's eyes snap open. "Rest now? I'm not dead."

"Didn't say you were!"

"Too right you didn't. I'll tell you when I'm dying."

"You'll tell me when you're dying."

"You'd better believe it."

I have to stifle my laughter. I get Wilf's attention and point upstairs. I'm going up to the belfry. I motion for him to lock themselves in, and then I'm out the door in a flash, rounding the final section of stairs.

I slow as I reach the last open door and the interior of the belfry comes into sight. It's a double-storeyed wooden structure. The top storey consists of a narrow walkway and handrail only, pressed against the walls of the tower, shutters letting in shafts of light from outside. Then there's a large central void where the bells and huge bell wheels hang, supported by heavy beams.

In the middle of all this is Kit.

He's all concentration as he sits on a wooden beam between the large bell wheels and scrapes over and over again at one of the bells. I know the words he's writing with the Waldram Raven's beak, because I wrote them myself in the scenes I drew, back in my bedroom in Chester Square.

When this bell rings, the human and faerie worlds will be divided once more. Forevermore.

If Kit, Wilf and Bes can pull this off, the London of the Bells will be no more. The Ravens will turn into ravens, the Londoners will awaken, and the Crown can return.

Finally, the connection between the faerie and human worlds will be broken.

I hold my breath as I watch Kit work, amazed at how all of this has come together so quickly – how no one has guessed before now, or talked about the possibility of this ending. Everyone was so caught up in the storming of the White Tower, including me. Of course, there were other theories – people who thought the bells might be turned on the Ravens somehow. That this would be fitting. Looking back, I think that was what the guy at the Bells Experience had been referring to, and it was what I'd looked up in the middle of book seven, back at the apartment. There was an incident where several of the fourteen bells were ringing at the same time, and their chimes were accidentally cancelled out by the ringing of a much older bell. It had been the smallest of bells. An inconsequential little handbell with a cracked wooden handle. But it was very old. Which meant that when it had been rung, all the other bells had silenced, listening to what it had to say. Bells are obedient that way. They are respectful of their elders.

That was the clue that had been left for me.

That I had left for myself, in a way.

Edie had left that small thought hanging. Dangling in the air like the clapper of an old, disused bell, biding its time, patiently waiting to be rung.

I'm sure lots of readers thought quite a bit about that little bell and the rules surrounding chiming, but maybe they also dismissed those thoughts when nothing came of it. It would be easy to do – after all, any bells outside the wall would be too far away to be heard by the others. But, just as the faeries could hear the bells chiming when I couldn't, of course the bells could hear each other, too. That is, they could feel each others' vibrations on the wind, from far, far away.

Perhaps even from this far.

That's what we're banking on here.

That and whether a beak that etches words onto a bell needs to be a *living* Raven's beak. That was another clue left behind for readers. Things always happen for a reason in a story, and Wilf knocking the Waldram Raven's beak to the floor in book eight had most definitely happened for a reason.

I slip into the belfry properly now, but hide in the shadows, against the stone wall. It's taking so long for Kit to inscribe the words that I know danger can't be far away. But to make the inscription shorter would have been a mistake. We needed to be sure. The worlds need to be divided once more. *Forevermore.*

Come on, Kit. Come on.

All I can think about is that slow death march of faeries and Londoners. The Ravens who are surely winging their way here.

Scrape, scrape, scrape.

If only I could help him. But I can't. I know I can't. I'm not supposed to be here. In this scene, Kit is on his own. And maybe he senses my presence and what I'm thinking, because he looks up to the walkway for a split second. He spots me in the shadows and his green eyes widen.

"Jeans!" he calls out and then grins.

I look down. My black skinny jeans are gone, replaced by blue ones. More changes! I run my hands down the front of them. What does it mean? What's Edie doing? I start to grin like Kit, but then stop myself. Not yet. I look back over at him to see what he thinks, but he's busy with his work again, knowing that every second is precious.

Scrape, scrape, scrape . . .

bash.

Both Kit and I jump at the unexpected sound.

It came from outside. From something beyond the wooden shutters – the ones directly across the void.

Kit scrapes at the bell faster. Harder. He leans so far over the bell wheel I'm scared he'll fall.

Bash, crash.

We both know what's out there making that noise. That's not just the lone Raven from before, but several flinging themselves at the shutters, trying to get inside.

So, this is it.

It's now or never.

Scrape, scrape, scrape.

Bash, bash, bash.

Kraah-kraah! Kraah!

And then another noise. From down the bell tower's stairs. A creak. A crack. A snap.

The chair.

It's the chair breaking.

The mob is inside.

COME on, Kit. Come on.

I have to put both hands over my mouth to stop myself crying out.

"Almost done!" Kit yells to Wilf and Bes below.

"Quit yapping and keep scratching," Wilf yells back, his voice muffled by the wooden floor.

Scrape, scrape, scrape.

Come on!

"Last word!" Kit yells.

My eyes are fixed on the shutters on the other side of the room. It's been too quiet for too long.

I've only just thought this when there's an almighty thud from outside. A terrible splintering of wood follows, above the awful screech of the Ravens.

A large black wing pushes through the shutters into the belfry, flapping wildly.

They're in. They're in!

The horrible wing beats frantically, faster and faster, stuck. I want to run across the walkway and push it from the window. But I can't. I'm not here. I can't help Kit. Instead, I sink further back against the wall. To give my hands something to do, I take the little Bes figurine out of my pocket and hold it tight.

Hurry, Kit, hurry.

The wing continues to beat, raising clouds of dust within the belfry. Meanwhile, the *kraah*ing of the other Ravens retreats. It's only a momentary reprieve. I know they're going to regroup and come back, and this time, there'll be no stopping them.

I turn my head towards the door. The noises on the stairs are getting louder. The mob is almost here. Kit is about to have a battle on two fronts and there is nothing I can do about it – it's all down to him now.

Scrape, scrape, scrape.

Flap, flap, flap.

I can't stand to watch that terrible flapping wing, so I close my eyes.

And that's when the shutters explode.

The noise is deafening – wood splitting and flying every which way. Three Ravens shriek as they tumble and spill into the room, hitting the walkway handrail and piling on top of one another.

Kit doesn't even look up. Instead, he concentrates even harder on scraping the final word onto the bell – making the best of the precious last seconds he has.

When the Ravens right themselves, they finally spot Kit below. When they spy the Waldram Raven's beak in his hand, they cronk throatily, incensed. They rise up and are on the handrail in a second, trying to get at him. But it's difficult. They're large, and while the belfry isn't exactly small, the Ravens need a certain amount of room to take flight, and there are three of them. They scrabble and scratch at each other, silver spurs flashing as they all try to take off at the same time. Wings flap and snap and the echo of *kraah, kraah-kraah!* bounces off the stone walls, the noise building and higher.

I cover my ears, eyes wide as I look on at the horrible scene. The Ravens hover above Kit, pecking and biting him whenever they get a chance. And all the while, he keeps scraping away, ducking and punching at the Ravens, trying to use the bell wheel as a shield.

Scrape, kick, duck, scrape.

Through the curtain of black feathers I see that Kit's bleeding now, his clothes torn. He has a terrible gash all the way up one arm, care of a Raven spur.

Scrape, scrape.

I gasp as one of the Ravens darts up and then shoots rapidly down, just missing Kit's face as he jerks to one side at the very last second. But just when I think Kit is okay, another Raven tries its luck. This one dives too low, hitting its head on the large bell wheel with a crack. The Raven falters, stunned. The dark beast drops, hitting the bell wheel and then sliding off, landing on its back on top of Kit. I gasp as he's crushed by the weight of the

Raven, his arms and legs thrusting out as he struggles to get up and complete his task.

With a shake, the Raven comes to, manages to right itself groggily and, after a moment, jumps on top of a beam, at Kit's level. It lunges for the beak.

Kit stabs at the Raven.

Once.

Twice.

Kraah!

It stumbles again and falls backwards, through the beams and beneath the bells, landing with a thump on the wooden floor below. It rights itself and attempts to fly upwards, but it can't. Too large to fly up through the beams, it's trapped. All it can do is peck hopelessly at the soles of Kit's boots.

One down, two to go.

Kit crawls back to the bell.

Scrape, scrape, scrape.

My eyes are wide as I watch the other two Ravens, perched on the handrail. They'd kept out of their brother's way as he fought with Kit, but now they ready themselves to attack once more.

Come on, *Kit!*

One Raven swoops, so cleanly and neatly that Kit is clipped around the head before he even hears it coming.

Kit looks dazed and wobbles on his beam. For a second I think he might fall off. But he doesn't.

He clutches onto the beam for a moment, steadying himself, then keeps on scraping.

Meanwhile, the Raven rises up, landing on the handrail again as the other Raven flexes his wings, ready for his turn.

I look at Kit in horror. I don't think he can take one more hit. Not like that.

Surely it's all over for him.

Scrape, scrape, scrape.

The Raven swoops.

Scrape, scrape.

Scrape.

But then a different noise makes my breath catch.

Tap.

Tap.

Tap.

Kit ducks, and the Raven hits the bell wheel with a thump at the very last second before flying off again.

"Now! Now! *Now!*" Kit calls out at the very top of his voice, above the *kraahs!* of the Ravens. Above the flapping of the trapped Raven on the floor below.

I hold my breath.

Nothing happens.

The bell is still. So still.

And the words upon it remain dark.

"Come on, come on, come on . . ." I whisper, urging the words to fizz aflame on the bell's surface. What's gone wrong? Maybe the bell knows the beak is from a dead Raven? Maybe the faerie magic won't work on the bells this far outside the wall? Maybe Kit hasn't etched the words in deep enough?

Maybe this is the wrong ending after all.

But then . . .

A spark. A glimmer, and the words begin to slowly light up, as if aflame, burning their fiery orange mark across the bell's surface.

When this bell rings . . .

The Ravens above and below let out an ear-splitting wail and launch themselves at the bell, trying to stop it from moving.

But they're too late.

The bell begins to drop. I watch the heavy clapper inside as it falls back in slow motion and, finally, strikes with a "ding".

It is the sweetest sound I have ever heard – will ever hear – followed by the most disturbing one, as the

Ravens cry out shrilly in defeat, shrivelling up before my very eyes.

I gasp as I watch them wilt and fade – two of them sliding to the floor of the walkway, the other now on the floor of the belfry itself. It flies up, fitting easily between the beams now that it's raven-sized, and comes to rest beside the others.

The three ravens look on from above as the bell swings backwards and forwards and begins to peal louder and louder.

Three normal, everyday ravens.

It worked.

It really worked!

The ravens sit for a moment, looking around, confused.

Kit pushes himself off the beam and clambers up the small ladder to the walkway. He is scratched and bleeding all over. "Get out of here," he growls at the ravens over the ear-splitting noise of the bell, chasing them off. "All of you. Go! Get out!"

The three ravens startle, flying around the room stupidly, bumping into the walls before finding their way to the broken shutters and exiting the tower.

When they're gone, Kit turns from the window and we look at each other. I'm guessing we're thinking the same thing. These Ravens might have changed form, but what about all the others?

Is it enough?

Has the bell's message reached London?

I don't know.

One thing I do know, however, is that I can still hear noises floating up the stairs from down below. We still have other guests.

The Ravens might be ravens, but the mob is still a mob. We're not done here yet.

I beckon Kit over. We stick our heads outside the door and try to listen over the bell.

There's another banging sound. Yelling.

It's definitely the mob, downstairs. I'm surprised they haven't come up here yet. I suppose they might not even suspect anyone's up in the belfry. If they've found the locked door of the room Wilf and Bes are in, they're probably focusing on that.

Kit pulls back for a moment and I can see he's trying to come up with some sort of plan. I grab his arm and shake my head. Whatever's going on down there, it's Wilf's turn to protect his friends and save the day. Just like Bes had before, and then Kit, just now. Loyal and true to the end. Kit seems to get what I mean, because he nods back. He goes to say something, but then his head whips towards the window. He runs across the walkway again and peers outside.

His ears are better than mine. He's heard something.

I hear it myself moments later.

A siren.

And . . . some kind of loudspeaker.

Several sirens and loudspeakers calling out a message.

I run over to stand beside Kit and look out the broken shutters.

There's a panicked crowd down below, spilling from St Lawrence's. Police cars. A fire truck.

I can only hear parts of the message that's being broadcast, but I get the gist of it.

Residents are urged to go home. Stay inside. Await further instruction. The wall has been breached.

The wall has been breached.

Kit points towards the street, and I realise people are spilling out of the church. The mob. The mob has heard the message and is leaving.

The wall is no more. The bell's message really did get through!

Kit whirls around and grabs me. We begin to jump up and down.

"The wall has been breached! The wall has been breached!" we chant as the bell begins to slow.

We've waited so long for this moment.

Been through so much.

But then I pull back.

This isn't my celebration. The ponytail, pink Converse and jeans have given me hope that Edie has plans for me, but we can talk about that later. This is someone else's story. Right now, Kit needs to be with Wilf and Bes.

He needs to be with the friends he's fought so hard beside, for so long.

His family.

"Go!" I yell at Kit, waving him off downstairs. "You need to go to them!"

But there's no need, because as he turns, Wilf and Bes burst into the belfry – Bes on Wilf's sturdy back. Wilf runs across the walkway, Bes jolting up and down as he goes.

I sidestep around Kit and scuttle across to the other side of the walkway, hurrying back to my dark corner. From there, I look on as Wilf carefully helps Bes down so the three of them can bring their arms up in their show of unity. Their arms touch for the briefest of moments before they collapse into each other, exhausted, hugging and crying, their foreheads together.

The bell quiets, having imparted its message, leaving Kit, Wilf and Bes in their own small world. Just the three of them in that circle of entwined arms. That's all that exists for them in this moment. All that matters in what was once the London of the Bells. And that is how it should be.

In the background, the wails of sirens and crowds heighten, floating upwards. Everyone thinks they're in danger, but the truth is, they've been saved by the trio huddled together across the room from me – the three bravest people I know.

Thanks to them, Ravens are ravens once more.

Bells are bells. Faerie magic has no channel into the human world. Only these three remain as a connection between the two worlds, and I can think of no three people I would trust more with that power.

I think of London. A freed London. Its people awakening. The Tower of London will be deserted now. Perhaps save for one lone raven, clinging to remembrance, waiting for his love, Princess Alice. Together, but forever apart.

A bittersweet ending.

Sad, but perfect.

It's as I watch the three of them that the thought enters my head. Loud, sharp and clear as the clang of one of the now-silent bells.

It's time to go.

I know without a doubt that it's Edie speaking. She's made her decision and it's time for me to leave. She has her ending. The one her characters wanted all along. An ending she is happy with. Her artistic battle with herself is over.

Just like that, my presence is no longer required in the London of the Bells.

I open my mouth, wanting to cry out. To argue. No! Wait! The changes – my shoes, my jeans, the ponytail. I'd thought it meant something. I'd thought Edie had some kind of plan for me. We all did. Those changes can't have been a mistake. Or maybe she meant every single one?

Maybe Edie had been trying to distance herself from me, knowing what she'd done. Knowing she'd created me and was then going to have to . . . get rid of me. I don't know. *I don't know.* I try to speak, to yell, but no words come out. I'm mute. Voiceless.

I try to wave my arms to get everyone's attention, but I can't move now, either. All I can do is stand in the shadows and await the fate that Edie has dealt out.

As I stand, still and silent, I attempt to fight the approaching darkness. I clutch on to my memories. I try to remember the good times I had here. Flying with Bes, the breeze in my hair and the Thames below me. Taking in the dancing reflections of light in Kit's grotto. Wilf telling me I have a bug in my teeth. My forearm pressed up against my friends' in solidarity.

I was real in those moments.

As real as anything.

I hold the little Bes figurine tight in my hand and replay those scenes in my mind.

"Wait. Tamsin. Where's Tamsin?" Bes calls out.

It's the last thing I hear as the blackness envelops me.

"TAMSIN!" I call out, trying to sit up. But I'm too weak. My muscles refuse to cooperate, my head spins, and I fall back onto my bed.

Which isn't my bed at all – it's a hospital bed.

"Edie." Someone bustles across the room to my bedside. "You're awake!"

It's Mrs Marchant, I see through blurry eyes.

"What's happening? What's going on?" I croak, then am overcome by a fit of coughing.

Mrs Marchant puts her hands gently on my shoulders. "Rest, Edie. You have pneumonia. I found you on the floor in your study. Do you remember?"

I shake my head.

But then . . . wait. I do remember. I remember seeing the doctor. Being warned that I was overtired. Stressed. And then the cold. Pneumonia. All the while trying to work. To finish book ten. I have to finish book ten.

"You were given strict instructions to stay in bed over the weekend. But I had a feeling you wouldn't do that, so I popped by on Sunday to check on you, and I'm very glad I did. I have no idea how long you were on that floor."

"I need a sketchbook. And a pen."

"You most certainly do not!" Mrs Marchant tuts.

"I most certainly do!"

"You're not well, Edie."

"You don't understand. I need to get this down. All of it. Before I forget. And I can't forget this. I can't."

Mrs Marchant frowns, staring deep into my eyes. She knows me. Too well.

And I might be an adult, but I am still a little bit scared of Mrs Marchant. That's why I call her Mrs Marchant, and not Emma. I force myself to stare back at her. Hard. I usually give in when it comes to Mrs Marchant. I often find myself bossed into taking breaks, and my 4:30 pm walk. But not this time. I narrow my eyes.

Finally, she sighs. "Oh, all right. I know you'll only expend more energy fighting me if I say no. But five minutes only. And if your doctor asks why you're working, I'm going to tell her it's completely against my better judgement."

"Five minutes is all I need," I tell her. And I think it's true. Five minutes is all I need to sketch this gift I've been given that is too precious to lose.

One week later

"Are you sure you're ready for this, Edie?" Mrs Marchant peers out my study window while Ink stands guard beside me. There's a sudden flash of light from a camera as a photographer notices the lace curtain twitch, and Mrs Marchant steps back. Ink, however, lunges forward with a hiss.

"I'm ready."

"Well, I don't know." Mrs Marchant gives me a look. "I think perhaps it's a bit soon."

"I really do feel much better," I tell her, adjusting my scarf.

Mrs Marchant accompanies me towards the front door of the townhouse. She's careful to close the study door behind us, closing Ink inside. We can't have him attack any more journalists.

"Hmmm ... you'd probably feel even better if you'd rested properly this last week. But we'll never know, will we?"

I can only grin at her as she steps forward and opens the front door wide, allowing me to step outside onto the portico.

Immediately, the flashes start. Voices call out as the journalists elbow each other for the best position.

"Ms St Clair!" One voice rises over the rest. "How are you feeling?"

"Much better, thank you."

"Is Ink locked up?" another journalist asks, making everyone laugh.

"Yes. We don't want any blood spilled today. There's been enough of that in the London of the Bells."

"Is it true that you've finished the tenth and final book?" another journalist bursts in.

I pause, toying with the loaded silence that follows. Sometimes being an author is fun.

"That is true," I finally say. "I handed it in to my editor yesterday evening. She was . . . much relieved."

The journalists chuckle. It's common knowledge that I was very late handing in book nine. So much so that my poor editor ended up moving into my house in the hope of hurrying me along. There was a long line of people waiting for that book.

"Are the rumours true that book ten is not only the final book in the *London of the Bells* series, but your last book ever? That you'll be moving on to other artistic endeavours now?"

Again, I pause. I wait for absolute quiet this time. When I could hear a pin drop, I smile. "That is . . . *not* true. I had considered moving away from graphic novels, but the fact is, while I was in hospital, I started another story. One that I'm very excited about."

The journalists immediately erupt in a frenzy of questions. I can barely understand anything I'm being asked.

"Can you tell us anything about it?" One journalist pushes forward from the pack. "Anything at all?"

She doesn't sound hopeful. I'm well-known for being extremely secretive about my work.

But this time she's in luck.

This time I *want* to share.

I clear my throat and the frenzy dies down.

"This book . . ." I begin, but then find I have to pause. Not for effect this time, but because snapshots begin to flash in my mind and I suddenly find the words won't come. Tears fill my eyes and I have to centre myself before I continue. "This book will be about a very special girl. A talented, brave, eleven-year-old artist who struggles at school, but at home is able to draw herself into her favourite fictional world."

"What's her name?" a lone voice calls out.

Another dazzling flash of remembrance. I see her standing as she landed in the hideaway that final time. Hands on her hips. Ready to write her own ending. Part of me, but all herself. But this time she isn't in the hideaway. She stands in the never-ending white room. Waiting for me. Waiting for her readers.

And I already know she will be loved. So loved.

She will be as real as anything.

I take a deep breath and ready myself to create the world she deserves to live in.

"Her name is Tamsin, and she's wonderful. She's so, so wonderful, and I can't wait for you all to meet her."

To Tamsin, the most real person I know.

– EDIE ST CLAIRE

ACKNOWLEDGEMENTS

Some novels come easier than others and this one did not come easily at all. A world within a world was always going to be a challenge and a challenge it was in both the writing and editing. Thanks to all who helped along the way. To Rob Ryan for the initial inspiration, which came on the cover of a gifted notebook. To my family who read early on (as per usual, the finished product does not at all resemble the version you read). To all at Walker Books Australia, who always seem to understand my strange little stories and help to turn them into what I actually wanted to say. To my agent Jordan Hamessley and all at New Leaf Literary. And to Allison Tait for her continued Zen and the art of publishing discussions.

ABOUT THE AUTHOR

Allison Rushby, the daughter of an author, was raised on a wholesome and steady diet of classic English literature. She has long been a fan of cities with long, winding histories, wild, overgrown cemeteries, red brick Victorian museums, foxes and ivy. She likes to write with a cup of Darjeeling tea by her side, a Devon Rex cat called Claudia curled up in her lap and puppy Harry at her feet. Allison's books with Walker include the middle-grade novels *The Turnkey*, *The Seven Keys* and *The Mulberry Tree*. You can read more about her work and upcoming books at www.allisonrushby.com.

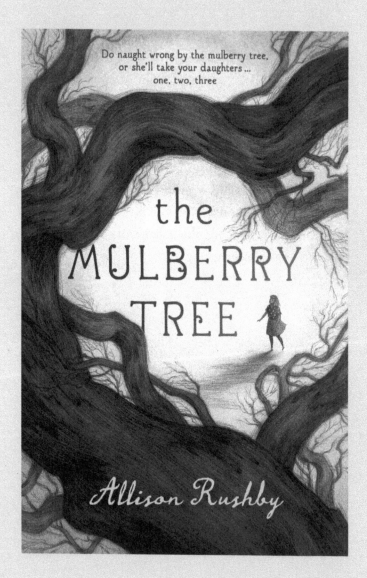

Do naught wrong by the mulberry tree,
or she'll take your daughters ...
one, two, three

the
MULBERRY
TREE

Allison Rushby

Do naught wrong by the mulberry tree,
or she'll take your daughters . . .
one, two, three.

Ten-year-old Immy and her family run away from their storm cloud of problems to a tiny village in Cambridgeshire, England. When they find an adorable thatched cottage to begin a perfect new life in, the only downside is the ancient, dark and fierce-looking mulberry tree in the back garden. And the legend that comes with it – the villagers say the tree steals away girls living in the cottage on the eve of their eleventh birthday. Of course, Immy thinks this is ridiculous. Then she starts to hear a strange song in her head . . .

Flossie Birdwhistle is the Turnkey at London's Highgate Cemetery. As Turnkey, Flossie must ensure all the souls in the cemetery stay at rest. This is a difficult job at the best of times for a twelve-year-old ghost, but it is World War II and each night enemy bombers hammer London. Even the dead are unsettled. When Flossie encounters the ghost of a German soldier carrying a mysterious object, she becomes suspicious. What is he up to? Before long, Flossie uncovers a sinister plot that could result in the destruction of not only her cemetery, but also her beloved country. Can Flossie stop him before it is too late?

Flossie Birdwhistle is the Turnkey at London's Highgate Cemetery. Seven years have passed since Flossie saved her country from a ghostly invasion during World War Two. Since then, things have been quiet. That is, until Flossie's nemesis, Hugo Howsham, reveals a secret the pair have been keeping – the keys of the Magnificent Seven cemeteries can be combined to make a Turnkey not only mortal, but immortal. When Hugo Howsham begins stealing keys, the other Turnkeys turn against Flossie, trusting her no longer. With family, friends and her cemetery in danger, can Flossie find the inner strength to protect everything she has ever cared about?

"This fine historical novel is an engaging and spirited sequel which will leave readers wanting more . . . Highly recommended."

– Read Plus